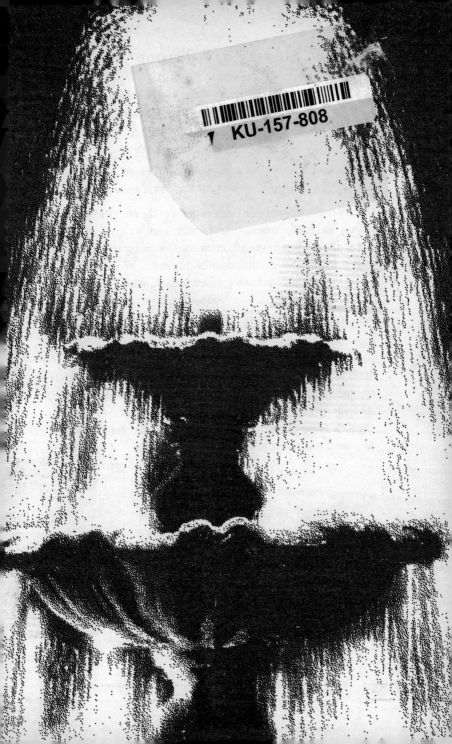

"Mendoza is a master of style, or styles (caught in Nick Caistor's translation) . . . With this novel, he presents a rural elegy and political fable and an adventure story all in one."

MICHAEL EAUDE, *T.L.S.*

"Unmistakeably Spanish in its characters and themes"

MARTIN ELLIOTT, *London Magazine*

"All the characters and relationships, not just the central one, are sharply and subtly drawn, while the nun, literally carried off her feet and on to a sofa by overwhelming lust (her own as much as her lover's) is a most skilful and sympathetic portrait of a woman in whom strength and weakness are inextricably tangled."

JOHN SPURLING, *Sunday Times*

"Mendoza spins a compelling tale of money, faith and love. In the 1950s, with memories of the Spanish Civil War still raw, a determined mother superior named Sister Consuelo, trying to raise funds to convert a nunnery's medical clinic into an old-age home, approaches a rich landowner in the Catalonian countryside. This innocent overture leads to untold complications for Sister Consuelo, who finds that her attraction for the wealthy Don Augusto is entirely worldly and utterly undeniable."

Publishers Weekly

EDUARDO MENDOZA was born in 1943 at Barcelona, where he now lives. He spent some years in New York working as an interpreter at the United Nations. After making his literary debut with *The Truth about the Savolta Case* (voted by *El País* one of the three best Spanish novels of the last fifteen years), he went on to write other novels, including *City of Marvels* which was selected by the Paris review *Lire* as "the best book we have read in 1988". His works have been translated into many languages and he is now considered one of Spain's most significant living writers.

Eduardo Mendoza

THE YEAR
OF THE FLOOD

*Translated from the Spanish
by Nick Caistor*

THE HARVILL PRESS
LONDON

First published in Spain with the title
El Año del Diluvio
by Editorial Seix Barral, Barcelona 1992

First published in Great Britain in 1995 by
The Harvill Press, 84 Thornhill Road, London N1 1RD

This paperback edition first published 1996

2 4 6 8 10 9 7 5 3 1

This edition has been translated with the financial assistance of the
Spanish Dirección General del Libro y Bibliotecas, Ministerio de Cultura.

© Eduardo Mendoza 1992
English translation © The Harvill Press 1995

Eduardo Mendoza asserts the moral right to be identified as the author of this work

A CIP catalogue record for this book is available from the British Library

ISBN 1 86046 045 3

Half title illustration of a fountain by Newell and Sorrell

Printed and bound in Great Britain by Mackays of Chatham

CONDITIONS OF SALE

THE YEAR OF THE FLOOD

I

DURING THE 1950s in the village of San Ubaldo de Bassora in the province of Barcelona there lived a wealthy man by the name of Augusto Aixelà de Collbató. He was the last of a long line of landowners, whose hard work, shrewdness and stubborn persistence had bequeathed him a noble family name together with a considerable fortune. Both of these seemed likely to disappear on his death, since at the time this story begins, and despite his being as old as the century, Augusto Aixelà was a confirmed bachelor. The bulk of his fortune came from an estate of around 300 hectares that sat astride the village boundaries of San Ubaldo (later absorbed into the town of Bassora) and Santa Gertrudis de Collbató, where one of the branches of his family tree originated. The ancestral home of this illustrious family, known to everyone locally as the "Aixelà house", was at the centre of the estate, the rest of which was given over to forestry and the growing of crops such as oats and alfalfa, although in the years immediately after the Civil War some land had been turned over again to vines, which produced a sharp, heady and low quality wine served from the barrel to working men in the wine cellars of Bassora. One summer afternoon, with the sun beating down, the small figure of a nun came panting up the road to the estate. Before reaching the crest of the hill, the nun paused for a few moments to get her breath back and to steady her nerves, because she was afraid she was in for a cool reception. At the top of the hill the track petered out at the wall surrounding the estate; beneath her lay the village of San Ubaldo, which in those days comprised scarcely a thousand souls, and beyond it the imposing mass of the hospital, the dry bed of the river, and the road which led through the village from Bassora to Collbató, where it joined the main highway to Barcelona. At that time of day the village seemed deserted; there was no-one in the streets, which twisted along the path of ancient streams or the boundary walls of properties that had long since disappeared. When the nun reached the main gate, she found it wide open. She looked for some way of announcing her presence, but when she could see no bell or person to call out to, strode purposefully across the threshold. She found herself on a broad, curving path bordered by tall lime trees, myrtle bushes and oleanders; a dense, shady garden hid the main house and its outbuildings, where the estate workers lived. The gravel path and the plants and trees in the garden showed signs of being carefully tended, but there was no-one to be seen or heard; the heavy silence of summer's most stifling hours hung in the air. The nun set off along the path; she had only taken a few strides when two huge dogs appeared round a bend, as if they had been lying in wait for her behind the myrtles. They looked fierce: the nun halted, closed her eyes and began to murmur: "Hail Mary full of grace". She could hear them panting and feel them sniffing at her habit. Then suddenly she heard a voice coming towards her, shouting: "León! Negrita! Get down!" She opened her eyes and saw a woman running along the path, crying out as she ran: "León! Negrita! Come here!" The dogs were still nuzzling her habit, growling and baring their fangs. When the woman came level with them, she gave them a hard slap on their backs and said: "Don't be frightened, sister, they won't harm you." She was a plump, cheerful-looking middle-aged woman, who wore a bloodstained white apron. The nun repeated her greeting

8

out loud, and the woman asked how she could be of service. The nun replied that she would like to see Señor Aixelà if he were at home and could receive her. "He's at home allright," the housekeeper said, "but I don't know if he can receive you or not: he's been shut in his office with the estate manager since this morning and has given instructions not to be disturbed." The nun nodded. "Please tell him that I am the Mother Superior of the Sisters of Charity who work at the hospital," she said, then added, with a wry smile: "And if you don't mind, take those dogs away, or take me somewhere where I don't have to see them."

A few lofty cypresses were interspersed among the lime trees; all of a sudden a goldfinch began to sing on an unseen branch. The dogs came ambling along behind the two women: they no longer appeared so hostile, and seemed to want to play. The nun kept a close eye on them all the same. The house was an old, long and uneven stone building, with a pitched roof, an arched front door and tall narrow windows like the loopholes of a castle. There was a sundial over the door, and on the lintel was inscribed a date that over the centuries had become illegible. On the flat stretch of ground between the track and the house, a holm oak cast its shadow on a battered old truck, painted green. A cat stuck its head out of the empty back of the vehicle. The woman explained that both truck and cat belonged to the estate manager. She added: "The master doesn't want the cat in the house because it's naughty and might break something valuable. Don't worry, it'll never get down as long as those two are around," she said, pointing at the dogs. She was doing all she could to be friendly to the nun and to make up for the poor impression the dogs must have made on her. "They're not fierce by nature," she had told her on their way along the path, "but it's their job to guard the farm, and they make no distinctions.

You know how bad things are in the region . . ." The nun did not know anything of the kind, but refrained from saying so: she was new to the area and to the position she held. She tried hard not to make her silence seem disobliging: she had no wish to offend this good, simple woman. "And yet the gate was open," she had commented in the end, in order to say something. The house-keeper had agreed: "The master says it is not doors that deter thieves, but the fear of what lies behind them." At right angles to the main house, but apart from it, stood a shed. At that moment a young man in a blue overall emerged from inside, a wooden pitch-fork slung over his shoulder. A cigarette butt dangled from his lips. When he saw the nun he stood the fork on the ground, took off his beret and stared at her, a blank, terrified look on his face. The dogs flopped down in the sun, panting and drooling; one of them rolled over in the dirt. "What stupid animals," the nun thought to herself as she made her way into the house. In contrast to the strong light outside, the hallway seemed plunged in darkness. "Wait here, will you, sister," the woman said.

Once her eyes had got used to the gloom, she could see that the only furniture in the room were a coatstand, four rush-bottomed chairs, and an old, rough-hewn trunk of the kind known as dowry chests. The room was far from welcoming. The housekeeper soon re-appeared and said, with an apologetic look on her face: "I'm truly sorry, sister, but the master cannot see you today. He says that if you wish to talk to him, you should come back on Thursday at the same time. I really am sorry," she added in a low voice. "No," the nun replied, "it was my fault for coming unannounced; you did all you could. I'm very grateful to you."

★ ★ ★

The nun returned to the farm on the agreed day. The same scene was played out with the dogs at the gate, but this time she did not come to a halt. Instead, she stared them in the face and muttered: "León! Negrita! Down!" and then set off determinedly down the path until the pair of dogs blocked her way, teeth bared, and cut short her exploit. The housekeeper, who came to her rescue when she had already retreated as far as the heather border along the estate wall, rebuked her: "Ah, sister, don't ever do that again – if they jump up at you, they could tear your throat out." Then she added: "It will be different when they get to know you." "When they get to know me?" the nun thought. Don Augusto Aixelà de Collbató received her in his study, offered her a cold drink, and apologised for what had happened a few days earlier. "I was caught up in some business I had to sort out there and then," he said, "and even if I had seen you, I could not have given you the attention that whatever brings you here doubtless requires." The nun believed she could detect a note of sarcasm in this solemn speech. "You will only get fine words out of me," seemed to be the message behind this bluster. "Yes, it is something important," she said firmly. Augusto Aixelà stared at her. He was tall and rangy, and despite his age carried himself with much of his former youthful grace. His hair was still black, and the lines on his forehead seemed due less to the passing of the years than to his permanent attitude of wry amazement. He assumed the air of a great landowner without much conviction: of late he had come to the conclusion that that was the role he should play, whether he wanted to or not. In fact, he would have liked to have been a cultured Madrid intellectual, arrogant and full of ready quips, but fate had decreed that he should be born and live in provincial Catalonia – a backward, sleepy place. It is worth noting in passing that he had personally done his bit to contribute to this situation, since soon after the start of the Civil

War he had obeyed the call of his noble lineage and his right-thinking ideas and had rushed to put himself and all he possessed in the service of the cause of our glorious leader, General Franco. Once the war was over, circumstances and his own lethargy had combined to reduce him to the state he now found himself in. As he was not only rich and single but an attractive man, who could on occasion be both pleasant and discreet, it was widely rumoured he had enjoyed idylls and adventures with women of widely differing age and status. The nun said: "You don't owe me any apology: I came here without making an appointment, which is something that's not done; the fact is, I could not think of any other way of getting in touch with you." "But there are several," he said: "Are you sure you wouldn't like a cold drink?" The nun looked down at her hands, unsure how to respond to his offer: she wanted to avoid any suggestion that this was merely a social call, but at the same time did not wish to appear austere, as if she were deliberately drawing attention to the fact that she was a religious. "Since you insist, I'll have a glass of water," she said eventually. Augusto Aixelà laughed. "Don't underestimate my hospitality, sister; I'll have you brought a glass of lemonade. The lemons from the orchard are so sweet they don't need any sugar: you'll see how much you like it." While he left the room to give the instructions, the nun sat stiff-backed on the edge of her seat, hands folded across her lap. She looked round the study without moving her head, noting the furniture and the different objects. The shutters were closed and the curtains drawn: although the darkness did lend the room a semblance of coolness, it also gave everything in it a lugubrious look. Unlike the hallway, the study had too much furniture and adornments. On the walls hung large dark paintings in clashing frames, small engravings, gilded brackets that supported worm-eaten carvings. All these objects seemed extremely precious; some of them were exceedingly ugly. The furniture was heavy and old-fashioned, and even in the dim light that merged everything into an indistinguishable mass, looked faded and in need of repair. "Now, let's see what is so important," Augusto Aixelà said, seating himself once more in the swivel chair behind his desk. He stared at the nun, intending to intimidate her: though polite by nature, he was sure he was about to hear an outpouring of sighs, stammered confidences, and laments, and the prospect dismayed him. The nun began by saying that she had been appointed less than a month earlier to the position of Mother Superior of the nuns who ran the hospital. As she said this, she pointed to a spot on the wall which she believed corresponded to the direction in which the hospital lay. The landowner nodded: he was well aware of the hospital, an archaic ruin built like a castle, on whose fake battlements the ashen features of some hapless patient or other could now and then be seen. The hospital stood on a piece of ground beside a dried-up riverbed. On its western side lay a poplar grove, which belonged to the hospital and provided it with a tiny income. This, together with grudging support from the local bishop and an occasional bequest, enabled them to scrape by. Augusto Aixelà's eyes instinctively sought out his chequebook. He made his contribution to the selfless work of the hospital every year, but always on fixed dates: Christmas Eve and Maundy Thursday, and he was not about to change that rule. But the nun was taking her time. At length she said: "Well, if you know the hospital, there's no need for me to tell you what state it is in: the building is literally falling to pieces and the installations are from El Cid's time; none of the nuns, myself included, have even the vaguest notion about medicine – if I were ever to fall ill, I would not wish to be taken there." Augusto Aixelà's interest was aroused by the rather impish note he thought he could detect in the nun's words. He looked more closely at this person sitting talking to him in a falsely demure way: her wimple framed the regular features of a bright, cheerful face. "She can't be as young as she looks if she has become a mother superior," he thought, "and she's not as silly as she is trying to appear: that's pure sham." The nun kept her eyes on the floor, but as she spoke her docility evaporated, and her voice took on a metallic ring which betrayed a brusque, authoritarian nature. "Fortunately," she went on, "all the hospital's defects will soon be a thing of the past, because the State, or rather the Social Security, is going to build a new hospital not far from ours. This hospital – the new one, I mean – will have all the latest equipment and of course a highly skilled staff. When that happens, the old hospital and its crew will sink without trace; and that's why I came to see you." A cold smile flitted across Augusto Aixelà's face; he had also heard of the new hospital about to be built in Bassora. Bassora, an industrial town of almost thirty thousand inhabitants, was only eight kilometres from San Ubaldo, and was expanding rapidly. "I'm not interested in buying the land," he said. The nun reacted sharply. "And I couldn't sell it to you even if I wanted to," she retorted, "but I haven't come with the intention of selling anything." She uncrossed her hands from her lap and put them on the edge of the desk; her manner now was resolute and virile. "Look, Señor Aixelà," she said; "It seems to me we could transform the hospital into a care centre – but of course, that doesn't mean anything to you – I mean, into an old people's home." She swallowed hard, then went on: "Let me tell you about the idea; I won't take up much of your time." Augusto Aixelà nodded in agreement. "The problem of our old people is serious, and it's getting worse all the time," she went on. "Until recently, families looked after their older members – grandparents lived with their married children and their grandchildren – but that doesn't happen anymore. Nowadays, young people leave to work in the towns, or even go abroad, and can't take their parents with them. Even if they could and wanted to, where would they put them? Before, family houses were big, but now people live in small flats where there is barely room for a couple and two children. There are no people in service anymore, and life gets more expensive day by day. Old people are a burden and, sadly, all families want to do is to get rid of them. Already there are two eighty-year-olds living on their own in the village; goodness knows how many there must be in a place like Barcelona. These old folk have no-one to look after them, they run the risk of all kinds of accident, and have to take care of all their own needs precisely when they most need attention. The health service can do nothing for them: if they fall and break a bone, they simply put it in plaster and send them home. If they get ill, the doctor prescribes medicine they do not know how to administer to themselves and which as often as not they forget to take. Old people have to buy their own food, cook it, keep their houses presentable, and wash their own clothes, but most of them cannot even manage to dress themselves so they can go out – some of them take over an hour to do something as simple as tying their own shoelaces. Even getting out of bed can require a huge effort; they doze all day, but at night find it impossible to sleep, they're scared by the slightest noise, and say the rosary over and over, counting the minutes until the sun comes up. I could go on, but I don't want to seem too grim." She fell silent, and recovered her composure. It was only then that she realised someone was standing next to her, and she gave a start. It was the housekeeper who had saved her twice from the guard dogs, and who was now offering her a glass of lemonade on a silver tray. "How beautifully you talk, sister," she exclaimed. "Leave us, will you, Pudenciana?" Augusto Aixelà said. The housekeeper put the tray on the desk and left the room pulling a face. "She doesn't like being called Pudenciana, even though it's her real name," Augusto Aixelà explained when they were alone together again. The nun drank the lemonade at a gulp, put the glass back on the tray, sighed a deep sigh and sat in silence until Augusto Aixelà prompted her: "Carry on, sister, I'm listening." So she took up her story again, in a calmer tone. "Converting the hospital is no easy task," she said, "apart from all the repairs, the rooms will have to be refurbished. The heating and water systems will have to be changed, and so will the bathrooms and the kitchens. All of which of course implies a considerable investment. I've mentioned my idea to several people: to the mayor, to the civil governor's secretary, who was kind enough to see me, and to someone close to the bishop. All of them listened with great interest. They all felt it was a good, even a praiseworthy, idea, but none of them showed the slightest inclination to get involved in the project in any concrete way: I mean, of course, by offering financial support. I have no doors left to knock at, Señor Aixelà."

Augusto Aixelà thought for a while and then, with the same serious air with which he had listened to the nun throughout, asked her: "What is your name, sister?" She answered that she was called Sister Consuelo. He went on staring at her, and asked if that was the name she used to sign cheques or accept bills of exchange with. She smiled. "No, for business transactions I have to use my secular name," she said. "Well then, what is it?" Augusto Aixelà pressed her. "I don't know if I can tell you," she replied. "You can and must," he retorted. "If I am not much mistaken, we are embarking on a business transaction – unless all this is a plan to save my immortal soul." This time it was Sister Consuelo's turn to laugh. "Oh no, that's your priest's responsibility; I'm only trying to get you to

Heaven in a roundabout way. But did I hear you say we were embarking on a business transaction?" "Yes, but I did not say we had brought it to a successful conclusion – and I still do not know your name." "Constanza, Constanza Briones," the nun whispered. "That's nothing to blush about," he said. "Did I blush?" she asked. "Yes." "It must have been the lemonade," she replied. "Don't tell lies, Constanza Briones, or you'll have to go to confession," he chuckled. When Sister Consuelo spoke again, her voice was serious, as if she were anxious to dispel the frivolous tone that had crept into their conversation. "So you'll help me?" she asked. "I'm not sure, I don't even know exactly what it is you are asking me to do. I don't think you just want a donation, do you? Have you done your sums?" The nun replied: "I've made some rough calculations. I haven't brought them with me, but I can send them to you." "No, bring them with you yourself, and we can study them at leisure. Tomorrow I'm busy all day: come on Saturday afternoon," said Augusto Aixelà.

2

S HE FOUND the gate open as before. On the other side of
the wall, she came across the lad she had seen coming out of
the shed a few days earlier. This time he was wearing a
broad-brimmed straw hat and was clipping the heather with a pair
of shears. The nun said hello, and he responded by breaking off
from his work and doffing his hat, but when the dogs came up
barking and threatening to attack her, he did nothing, simply
replacing his hat, turning his back on them, and resuming his snip-
ping of the bushes. He must be one of those idiots they have on
every big estate, the nun thought: they carry out all the menial
tasks, they're very faithful and trustworthy, but you can't ask them
to take any responsibility. All the while, the dogs were doing their
duty with their usual ferocity: let's bark, leap about and show that
we'll bite to earn our keep, they seemed to be saying. Pudenciana
ushered her into Señor Aixelà's study, which was empty. "The
master won't be long," the housekeeper said. "I know you're not
fond of your real name," the nun said, "but tell me what I can call
you." "You can call me whatever you like, sister," replied the other
woman. "What do other people call you?" Pudenciana thought for
a moment. "Almost everyone calls me Cootie," she said eventually.
"I'm not sure you get the best of the bargain," Sister Consuelo put
in, "but if that's what you want, it's fine by me." "That's what I was
christened," said Pudenciana somewhat incongruously. The study
was as gloomy as it had been on the previous occasion, but this time

Sister Consuelo could make out a strange smell, a mixture of dust, wood and eau-de-cologne. When Pudenciana left her, she began to walk round the room, still clutching the file she had brought. She peered at all the weird and wonderful objects, and came to a halt in front of one of them. It was a wooden sculpture about a foot high, which must have been the figure of a saint, though the body was slightly deformed and twisted, as if it had been sculpted from the stock of a vine. There were traces of a faded plum-coloured paint on the base of the statue; one of the arms had come off, and in the other the saint was holding a rectangular object which looked like a box of sweets. He had a wispy beard, his eyes were rolled up, and he was gazing skywards in a lost fashion as though he were drunk. The overall impression was comic rather than pious, and the nun shrugged. She understood nothing about art, and had no wish to: it seemed to her wrong that objects of devotion should become museum pieces or collectors' items. "It's from the eleventh century, or perhaps even earlier," a voice said behind her. Sister Consuelo dropped her file and Augusto Aixelà immediately bent down, picked it up and returned it to her. "I'm sorry," he murmured, "I didn't mean to startle you." "I didn't hear you come in," she said, "I didn't even realise the door had opened." "No, it didn't," said Augusto Aixelà, "but don't worry, I haven't come through the wall either. I came from behind that curtain over there. And as for that statue, I've been told it comes from Saint-Martin de Canigou. It was one of the many treasures which left France during the Second World War. It's supposed to be an apostle, perhaps Saint Simon, although that's hard to say because as you know the saints' attributes only became part of the iconography in the fourteenth century. It's probably a fake anyway. Come this way," he said, pointing to the curtain from behind which he had appeared. He drew it back, and the nun followed him out onto a veranda which ran the whole length of the back of the house, offering shade from the sun. Beyond the veranda lay a somewhat overgrown garden, with a huge bushy fig tree and an acacia. Under the fig tree stood a round marble-and-iron table, which looked seldom used. A ripe fig had burst on the table top, and a cloud of flies swarmed over it. "I'll get them to bring you some lemonade," he said, and cut short her gesture of protest by saying: "Giving a drink to someone who's thirsty is an act of charity, so do not deny it to me." There was no trace of sarcasm in what he said, so the nun smiled. He motioned for her to sit in one of the two wicker armchairs on the veranda. She did so, and he disappeared into the house. A warm breeze wafted the smell of the fig tree over to her. Sister Consuelo took a deep breath: at the bottom of the garden, beyond a row of clipped cypresses, she could make out a vegetable garden, with a pond at the far end. Further on still, the land rose in terraces planted with vines. From her vantage point, she could even make out the bunches of grapes. So absorbed was she in contemplating all this that she jumped once more when she realised that Augusto Aixelà was standing beside her again. "I'm behaving like a schoolgirl," she thought, but she said: "What a pleasant spot." "Yes, I usually spend summer evenings here, when-ever I'm free. It's a really beautiful estate, and not just in the literal sense of the word. I mean it's well-run, with real skill: I can say that without blushing, because it was true when I inherited it. I have simply tried to keep it up and to follow my ancestors' guidelines." He breathed in deeply and added: "I love this estate more than anything else in the world, but what will become of it when I die?" The nun glanced at him anxiously: she had come to talk about her worries, not to listen to someone else's. Before she could say anything, however, the landowner made as if to brush away an insect flying round his face, and then looked directly at the nun with a broad smile on his face, as if his gesture had also managed to sweep away his melancholy. "Are you from the countryside, sister?" he asked. His question was tactfully put, and Sister Consuelo nodded. "Yes," she said, "my parents were country people who had managed to save some money. They were not educated or cultured, but they were as honest as the day is long, and god-fearing. It was thanks to their efforts and understanding that I was able to study to join the church, and then later to offer a dowry to our Order." When she came out with the lemonade on a tray, Pudenciana found them absorbed in their conversation. "While you're drinking it," Augusto Aixelà said when the house-keeper had left them alone once more, "I'll have a look at those figures of yours." "Let me explain them to you," she said. "No," he replied, "figures are often much clearer than words, and less argu-mentative. You drink and take a rest. After the walk you've had in this heat and with that idiotic habit you're wearing, I'm amazed you haven't fainted already." Sister Consuelo said nothing: at that moment she felt carried away by an extraordinary lightness, bordering on intoxication, as though the sense of wellbeing and peace she enjoyed in this gentle landscape, so different from the arid track she had climbed, had thrown her off balance. Tearing her eyes away from the greenery she saw, at the far end of the veranda, a parrot chained to a hoop. She turned to Augusto Aixelà to ask about the presence of this unusual bird, but he had put on a pair of wire-framed glasses and seemed caught up in his perusal of the file, so she got up and went to look more closely at the parrot. She had never seen one before, and it seemed to her both exotic and disturbing. Its beak and claws were sharp and threatening; its round eyes had a blank, malevolent stare; but its plumage looked so soft and brilliant that it contradicted the danger inherent in its fierce traits and turned the bird into a thing of luxury. The nun was fascinated by this strange juxtaposition. "It doesn't talk, but it could," Augusto Aixelà commented. Sister Consuelo was disturbed to realise she was being watched, and turned in the direction of the voice she heard. Augusto Aixelà was still sitting in his chair, with the file open on his lap. He had not taken off his glasses, and the lenses magnified his eyes, turning them into two glassy protuberances that matched the parrot's inhuman gaze. "I'd never seen one before," she said lamely, as if she felt she had to justify her curiosity. He left the file and his glasses on the table by the chairs and came over to join her. Seeing itself the centre of attention, the parrot fluffed out its feathers, opened its beak, and let out a piercing squawk. "The person who gave it to me," Augusto Aixelà said, "told me it came from the Amazon jungle, like all those of its kind. They're caught there and sent to Europe in cargo boats. On the journey they learn to repeat everything the crew say: a jumble of curses and obscenities that later scandalise their owners, because they never forget what they have learned by chance. But this fellow never seems to have learnt anything, perhaps because when he was brought over he was kept apart from the others, and never heard any human voices. I ought to teach him something, but I don't have the time or the inclination: I'm a hopeless teacher." The nun left off contemplating the bird, and the two of them went back to sit in their chairs. They sat for a while in silence, staring into the distance, as though assessing the garden and the vineyards. Finally the nun said: "Well, what do you think?" Augusto Aixelà turned slowly towards her. "I've only had time to glance at the project," he said, "but I can assure you that the figures do not match." "Match what?" she wanted to know. "Your intentions," he replied, "or reality. You talk here of two million pesetas, but to my mind to carry out what you are proposing you would need far more than that: four million, or five, or even more, I don't know. Where did you get the figures from?" "Oh, from here and there," she replied evasively. "They're wrong," he said, "wrong and incomplete. For a start, you haven't included the cost of labour anywhere in your budget." "No, because I didn't think it was important," Sister Consuelo hastily said, "in fact, we could do it all ourselves, we are not frightened of hard work." Augusto Aixelà shot her an irritable glance. "It doesn't frighten you because you don't know what it is," he growled. Sister Consuelo stared at him, taken aback, and he went on: "I'm a man of few convictions, but experience has taught me to value work above everything else. You treat it lightly perhaps because you are confusing work and effort: work is effort of course, but it is also knowledge and persistence. It is not a matter of using brute strength against matter, but of knowing what one wants to achieve and why, and how this is to be done; and then carrying out that task laboriously, intelligently, with love, and with centuries of dedication and purpose behind one's every gesture." He stood up and walked off down the veranda, while the nun sat astonished. All of a sudden, although it had seemed he had nothing more to say, he stopped and pointed at the hill. "Look at that garden and the vineyards," he said. "The earth here is dry and the rainfall is unreliable, but they flourish thanks to an ingenious, complicated system of wells, irrigation channels and sluices that controls the flow of water to them. The system is so ancient that no-one knows who invented it or put it into practice or when, even though everything related to the estate has been documented for over six hundred years. Everything you can see, and everything that can't be seen, from those terraces to this house, from the lemonade you have just drunk to I myself, all of us are the product of that immense, uninterrupted and anonymous effort." He came back to the table, closed the file, and gave it back to the nun. "Here you are; I know you acted from the best possible intentions, but I can't take your fantasies seriously. The governor and the bishop were right not to listen to you. They are well-bred people, so they were more polite about it, but I'm just a country clodhopper and you'll have to forgive my being so blunt and to the point." Sister Consuelo sat in silence for a while, then glanced down at her watch and muttered an excuse: it was Saturday and she had to attend the evening prayers. She stood up, bowed to him so formally it seemed almost like a curtsy, then left with her eyes fixed on the ground, and the file clutched to her.

And yet a fortnight later, the same nun climbed the hill up to the farmhouse, with the same file under her arm. The dogs went through their usual ferocious song-and-dance. "I don't expect Señor Aixelà wants to see me," she told the housekeeper, "but if he agrees to do so, I will only keep him a minute." "I'll tell him at once, sister," she replied with what seemed to Sister Consuelo like a flash of panic on her face. Perhaps she heard the way he scolded me the other day and is frightened there'll be an even bigger row this time, she thought. She is wrong though: however much he gets at me, I won't budge an inch. I must keep my humility at all costs, that is my duty. But the landowner greeted her with a friendliness that was almost condescending. "I came to apologise for the way I left the other day," she said before he had time to speak: "I was confused, and I did not manage to thank you for your sincerity." "You have no reason to apologise," he said, "I was really pretty savage, and you reacted quite appropriately." "I would also like to thank you," the nun interrupted him, "for what you term your savagery. What you told me was not only correct but obvious, but it is something which out of pride and stubbornness I would never have understood if you had not said it as forcefully as you did." "In that case," he said after a short while, "we're at peace." "But it's only a truce," Sister Consuelo replied, a faint smile in her eyes and on her lips. "I see you've brought the famous file again," he said. "I've been checking the figures," she explained. Augusto Aixelà laughed out loud. "Come on, let's go out onto the veranda," he said, pulling back the curtain. "I'd like you to take another look at the budget, if it is not asking too much of your time and patience," said the nun. They were sitting in the wicker chairs again; Augusto Aixelà took the file from her and pulled his glasses case from his pocket. "No, of course it isn't," he said while he put on the glasses; "the fact is, your persistence amuses me – and I don't mean to insult you in any way by saying that," he hastened to add, "I say it with affection. You know we wouldn't be out here if I didn't respect your ideas and the boldness with which you are trying to carry them out." "I've gone through the figures," she said, cutting him short, "and I've sketched out a possible way to finance it. I'm convinced that if we could only raise the initial amount shown here, it would be easy to get official help: once things were under way, they wouldn't leave me in the lurch." "Let's see," he said, opening the file. In order to hide the agitation she felt at the situation, and the effort she was making to keep the difficult balance between appearing meek but at the same time firm, the nun got up and went to look at the parrot. The bird was performing a monotonous dance on its hoop: it hopped from one foot to the other, swaying its head to and fro. The repetitive movement looked both stupid and mesmeric. When the nun had come up level with it, the parrot opened its beak and screeched: "Hail Mary full of grace." Sister Consuelo burst out laughing, then recovered her composure and blushed. "Were you so sure we would meet again?" she asked. "I hope you're not offended," Augusto Aixelà said, without raising his eyes from the budget figures. "It was only a bit of innocent fun." "No, I'm not offended, but do you really think I'm so stubborn?" "Yes, but what's wrong with that?" he replied: "Stubbornness is no more than a way of approaching things: it can be used for unworthy aims, but also worthy ones." He shut the file and said: "Why do you think I can be of help to you?" "That's easy," she said, "because you have the necessary means." "Who told you I am rich?" Sister Consuelo lowered her eyes and murmured: "These things get around." "But you have only been here a month," he retorted; "look me in the eyes and tell me the truth: who has told you about me?" "Lots of people: the patients at the hospital, the doctors who come there, our suppliers, just about everyone; in such a small place these things are soon known." "But not all of them are true," replied Augusto Aixelà. "No, but there's some truth in all of them," she said. "What else have you heard about me?" he asked. "Nothing that is worth repeating," the nun replied. "Why? Are you only interested in my money?" "I'm only interested in facts," the nun replied, "I leave moral judgments in the hands of the Almighty." "I wasn't talking of judging, but of believing," he said; "you have heard things about me, and now my question is: Do you believe them?" "What does it matter to you what I believe?" Sister Consuelo protested. "It matters, and that's all there is to it," he said sharply. The nun clasped her hands on her lap, tilted her head and stared at her companion with an intensity that belied the modesty of her posture. Eventually she said: "I am a nun. I have devoted my life to prayer and to caring for the sick; I know very little of anything else, and have no wish to do so. It is true that I have heard a lot of things about you – some of them good, some of them bad. I have no reason to doubt the good things; the others reached me in the form of malicious gossip, so I do not necessarily believe them, although I know they are possible – all of us are capable of both good and evil." She swallowed hard and went on: "At any rate, if the unworthy acts people blame you for are true, there is nothing I can do apart from praying for the Lord to enlighten you, and that is what I do." "What! You pray for me?" "I pray for many people." "But for me as well." "Yes, you as well," the nun said. "That is my duty . . . and also my inclination. But I want one thing to be clear: When I pray, I pray to God. I hope you understand what I am trying to say." "Leave the file with me," Augusto Aixelà said all of a sudden, as if he suddenly found the conversation tedious. "I have to see my estate manager tomorrow and I'd like him to have a look at the figures, if that is all right with you. He's a very discreet and trustworthy person, and very good in practical matters." "Of course," she said in an almost inaudible voice. He added: "I'm leaving the day after tomorrow. I have to go to Madrid on a fairly important piece of business, and you know how these things are: I have no idea how many days I'll be gone, but as soon as I am back, I'll let you know." "I look forward to hearing from you," Sister Consuelo said stiffly, as if it required a great effort for her to talk; and yet, when the two met again in that same spot a week later, they were completely at ease with each other.

3

THE WEATHER was still extremely hot, and the clouds which partly covered the scorching afternoon sky only made the heat all the more stifling. As the wind pushed them across the heavens, their dark shadows flitted over the fields; the vine leaves took on a glint of steel. The nun expressed her interest in Augusto Aixelà's trip and the outcome of the business that had taken him to the capital. He told her the journey had been a real torture, that the train had suffered the usual delays and had finally deposited him, exhausted and covered from head to foot in soot, in an impossibly torrid Madrid. The streets were deserted; the melted asphalt stuck to the soles of everyone's shoes. Fortunately, he added, the lobby of the hotel he was staying in had efficient – perhaps too efficient – air conditioning. As for the rest, he went on, he had reason to think that the matter which had led him to take such a hasty trip was well on the way to being successfully resolved. In short, he concluded, despite all the discomfort, the journey had been worthwhile. "It's obvious," he said, "that your prayers were with me." "My prayers could hardly have had any influence on matters of which I know absolutely nothing," the nun replied. "You may not, but God does," Señor Aixelà retorted, "and perhaps the Almighty decided that since there is little he can do to save my soul at this point, he should use your prayers for more worldly ends." "Do not mock the effect of prayer," the nun said, "or try to shock me, because you won't succeed. I know that deep down you don't believe any of that, but I also know from experience that when they are faced with a nun's habit, all men feel obliged to come out with some idiotic comment or other." "Just as you do to scold me like a child," Augusto Aixelà replied, "but let's not start arguing: tell me what's been happening in that wretched hospital of yours while I've been away." The nun took a sip of the lemonade Pudenciana had served her a short while earlier, settled in her wicker chair, sighed, and said: "Not much, really; on Tuesday, due to an unforgivable oversight by our sister Doorkeeper, one of our mentally disturbed patients managed to escape from the hospital and went to the games room at the Ateneo Club. He spent two hours there playing billiards, dressed in his pyjamas and slippers, without anyone paying him the slightest attention. It's amazing how in a village where everyone is so curious about their neighbour's private life, the real situation people find themselves in arouses so little interest. Apart from that picturesque incident, there's little to report: This year, as ever, the dreadful drought is threatening to ruin our fruit crop; and we have missed having news from you." "In Madrid I was told the temperatures were the highest this century," Augusto Aixelà commented. "At noon one day I took a taxi in the Calle de Alcalá, but I had to get out half way, because there was no air to breathe inside the cab." "Did you do as you promised," the nun wanted to know, "did you show my plan to your manager?" "I did more than that," the landowner replied. "In Barcelona I took the liberty of making a photostat copy of your papers, and took it with me to Madrid in the hope of being able to do something with it there. And in fact it turned out that while I was busy in the corridors of the Interior Ministry on my own business, I bumped into a former university colleague of mine who now holds an important position in the Health Service. Of course I wasted no time in telling him of the project, and he seemed interested. The next day, a messenger came to my hotel to pick up the copy I had made, and even as we speak, your fantasies are probably in the hands of the Director General himself. So you can see, there is no reason for you to scold me." "Nor for you to doubt the efficacy of prayer," she said, her eyes veiled in tears. Then she recovered, quickly wiped the back of her hand across her eyelids, and said: "Is it true you did that for me?" "As I told you," he responded, "it was a worthwhile journey – and I even found time to visit an antique shop that for some reason was not closed for holidays, and bought a very interesting piece: would you like to see it?" The nun lowered her gaze and sat in silence for a few moments, then said: "I'd be delighted, but it will have to be some other time. It's late and there are still things I have to do for the hospital." "Let me take you in my car," Augusto Aixelà said. "No, please don't bother," replied the nun in a whisper. "I've already taken too much advantage of your kindness, and besides, the walk downhill is not tiring." As she was leaving, she paused in the doorway. "I do not know how to thank you," she stammered. "There's no need for you to do so," Augusto Aixelà said, "but are you feeling all right?" "Yes, yes, I'm fine, I assure you," she replied, "I'm just a bit flustered by what you've told me. It's difficult sometimes when you set your heart on something not to get carried away by your emotions. I know it's childish." She left the study and crossed the bare hallway, but as she was about to step into the garden, the sun struck her full in the face. She did not notice the step, stumbled, and would have fallen if a strong pair of arms had not grasped her. She turned to look, and saw the gardener's puffy face and felt his wine-sour breath on her cheek. He held her firmly, but not roughly, and his expression seemed to have lost all trace of idiocy. As soon as the nun had steadied herself, he let her go and stood a few paces from her, holding his cap respectfully in his hand. "Thank you, the sun dazzled me and I didn't see the step," she said. She set off down the path and he followed her; freshened by the recent rain, the plants were so lush they gave the place the air of a jungle, almost threatening. "You don't need to come with me, I know the way," the nun said. But the idiot followed her footsteps, speeding up whenever she did. His broad smile showed a perfect set of white teeth. Merciful God, the nun thought to herself, please let nothing happen to me. No sooner had the thought crossed her mind than she ran into the two fierce dogs. "Don't be afraid," the idiot muttered, and she understood that he had only come with her to protect her from them. "Are you from the hospital, sister?" he asked. "Yes," she replied. "Ah," he said, "they do good works there, good works."

A few days later torrential rains hit the whole of Catalonia, causing extensive damage in and around Bassora. The village of San Ubaldo did not escape the catastrophe: in a few hours, the trickling stream which marked the hospital's western boundary grew into a raging torrent that burst its banks at several points, flooding the crops and spreading across fields and along tracks, sweeping a variety of strange objects along with it and depositing them hither and thither in the countryside. A further result was that the operating theatre in the hospital was flooded. Sister Consuelo, who spent all her free time absorbed in the task of adjusting and perfecting the figures in her budget, was interrupted by Sister Francisca on behalf of all the community; the look on her face suggested the end of the world was at hand. "There's a foot of filthy water in the operating theatre," she said. Sister Consuelo did not even raise her eyes from her file. "Well then, mop it up and then make sure you disinfect the floor with bleach," was her only comment. Sister Francisca still hovered at the entrance to the cell. "What's the matter, sister?" Sister Francisca cleared her throat: "It would be best

31

if you came to see for yourself, reverend mother," she whispered. A dozen nuns were crowded on the staircase leading down to the operating theatre, terrorstruck; they had rolled up their sleeves and gathered up their habits, carried floorcloths and buckets, but stood there motionless. "Sisters, get to work with the buckets," Sister Consuelo urged them. Seeing her words had no effect, she set off down the steps and peered into the operating theatre: the lighting had been switched off to avoid a shortcircuit, so the only brightness came from a few narrow skylights in the tops of the walls. The whole floor was a chocolate-coloured lake in which she could see the operating table floating upside down. All the trays for surgical implements were also floating in the disgusting liquid. Cloths, compresses and an ether mask swirled around. Sister Francisca's trembling finger picked out one particular object among all the floating debris. It was a dead rat. "Is that what you are all so afraid of?" the Mother Superior called out. "Get rid of it at once, Sister Francisca, if you please." Sister Francisca rolled up her eyes like a martyr being thrown to the lions. "Didn't you hear me, sister?" "It gives me the shivers, reverend mother." At that, the Mother Superior strode into the water, picked up the dead rat by its tail, and handed it over to Sister Francisca. "Take it," she told her imperiously; "even though rats may be disgusting, they are God's creatures: throw it into the dustbin, but without any fuss." She thought for a moment and then said, from the top of the stairs: "I hereby determine that this operating theatre be closed until further notice, for a number of reasons, some of them relating to hygiene, others to technical matters; from now on, until the new hospital at Bassora is opened, anyone who needs an operation will have to take a coach into the city." This was the drastic news which greeted the hospital doctor when he arrived a couple of hours later, in a state of great excitement. Breathlessly the doctor related to a gaping-mouthed, anxious ring of nuns and patients the dramatic effects of the storm on the centre of Bassora, where he lived, and from where he had succeeded in escaping only after overcoming a thousand obstacles. Everything had begun, he told them, on the stroke of midnight, when the rushing waters had burst through the containing wall which channelled the river's passage through the town. As a result of this, a large number of manufacturing or commercial establishments situated on the banks of the canal precisely so they could use the water and tip rubbish and industrial waste directly into it, found themselves flooded or had collapsed, in either case suffering irreparable damage. In the town centre, the doctor went on, the flood had been even more spectacular: the rushing torrent had uprooted most of the trees, the street lighting, and the public benches, and swept away everything that lay in its path, in particular all the parked cars. It had also lifted or undermined vast sections of road. All the drains had burst, filling the streets and squares with all kinds of filth. The houses in some neighbourhoods, especially the new ones built in the lower part of town, had been flooded, forcing the people living there to seek refuge in the upper storeys or even on the roofs. Several elderly or invalid persons had been evacuated out of their windows. The gallant fire service was overwhelmed by so many emergencies, but since the roads out of town were blocked and the situation in the surrounding villages was just as bad, there was no possibility of receiving help from outside. On top of all this, the downpour had brought down almost all the electric cables, and smashed the drinking-water pipes; there were no telephones, so the town was in darkness, cut off from the world. These further calamities had made the rescue efforts even more difficult; they had been carried out in conditions which the doctor, who had not been present at the scene but who had heard a detailed account of what had happened

33

from an eyewitness, had no hesitation in qualifying as "Dantesque". In the darkness, he said, heart-rending cries and pitiful calls for help could be heard from places where the storm had caused the most damage. By three in the morning, the doctor continued, the tireless firemen, with the help of volunteers, had managed to evacuate all the inhabitants of El Arenal, a working-class neighbourhood where the houses were in grave danger of collapsing. Despite all this, he told them, the number of victims had been much smaller than the scale of the disaster had at first led everyone to expect: so far only two deaths had been reported. Two women, one a youngster of around fifteen, the other in her sixties, had drowned in the gypsy camp set up on the riverbank on the outskirts of the town. In another incident, two more women, a mother and her daughter, had been about to meet the same fate as the wall they had sought refuge on began to crumble, but they had been saved in the nick of time. In any case, the doctor added solemnly, as soon as daylight had permitted, the rescue teams had started the painstaking process of searching through the remains of the ruined houses, since there were fears that more people might be buried there. The homeless families had been put up in schools and other public buildings until, for lack of space and in order to ensure that nobody was left in the open, it became necessary to use the stalls and even the foyer of the Avenida cinema, from which a large poster of Marilyn Monroe in a provocative pose was removed as a mark of respect. It was heart-rending, the doctor went on, to see the distress of these unfortunate people who had so suddenly lost all they owned, who had seen all the possessions they had spent long years of sacrifice accumulating swept away by the waters in a few seconds. Snatched from sleep, they had been forced out of their houses in the middle of the night in their nightdresses or pyjamas, and now there were scarcely enough mattresses or blankets for

34

them all. In mid-morning, the radio informed those who had electricity that an aid convoy had been despatched promptly from Barcelona, led by His Excellency the Civil Governor, the provincial head of the Falange movement. However, the radio noted, the progress of the convoy, which was bringing food, medicine, clothing and other essential items to the flood victims, was seriously hindered by the state of the main roads which in some places, according to the radio announcer, whose voice trembled with emotion to convey the awesome nature of the spectacle "looked exactly like swiftly flowing rivers". There is no doubt that this year will go down in history as the year of the flood, the doctor said, moved by his own account, which he ended by referring to the difficulties he himself had had to face to reach the hospital, since the floodwaters had destroyed one of the bridges on the local road and he had been forced to make a long and arduous detour. As for the Mother Superior's decision to close the operating theatre indefinitely, the doctor said he had no objection; in fact, he warmly welcomed it – he had only a couple more years until retirement, and he found the responsibility of being the hospital's chief medical officer too onerous. The less work and the less responsibility the better, he thought to himself. These dramatic events forced Sister Consuelo to realise just how far in recent weeks she had been caught up in her plans for remodelling the hospital, putting her fantasies before the pressing needs of the present. "I only live for my dreams," she said to herself, "I can't go on like this." She at once put her figures to one side, and devoted all her time and energy to the hospital. This change in attitude, brought about by the drama already mentioned, which was amply covered in the press at the time, did her the world of good, forcing her out of a state of nervous anxiety that had lasted for several weeks. She had been restless the whole time, and had shown herself extremely irritable and demanding of her subordinates. What's wrong with me? she asked herself, I'm becoming unbalanced. Her mood changed constantly: she would wake up at first light full of a sense of extraordinary wellbeing such as she had never felt in her life before; but then a few moments later, when she became fully awake, she would fall prey to doubts and inexplicable worries, and had to appeal to all her common sense to avoid bursting into tears for no apparent reason. These moments of extreme contrast, first feeling she was being transported to the heights of delight, then immediately falling into the depths of despair, occurred throughout the day in the most unexpected and embarrassing manner. Sister Consuelo could find no reason for being so ill at ease, and since she saw nothing in it to reproach herself for, she did not mention it to her confessor - who anyway would have been of little help to her. He was an elderly priest, born locally, by the name of Father Pallares. He had spent the whole of the Civil War running away or in hiding, and all the commotion had affected his mind. He liked to tell the story of how in the early days of the war, to avoid the patrols searching for him house-to-house, he had hidden in an empty tomb in the cemetery, which two kindly persons had sealed with the stone, promising they would return and release him as soon as the danger had passed. The poor priest spent two days and two nights in that awful spot, with no food, almost no air, and in total darkness. He could not lift the stone on his own, and he was afraid that his two rescuers might have been taken prisoner themselves, or had fled the village, had betrayed him, or even might have forgotten exactly which tomb he was hiding in. He was cowardly by nature, and too old to withstand this kind of experience; as he saw it, he had never done anyone any harm, and knew personally all the republicans who were trying to find and kill him; he had seen many of them born, and had baptised most of them. The horror of his situation was made even more terrible by the sudden discovery of this unsuspected side of human nature, this abyss of loathing, of ancestral hatred. This so filled him with sadness that at times he felt he would have preferred to stay permanently in the world of the dead where he was being offered temporary shelter. It is only here that peace can be found, he thought. Nor had the years that had passed since then done anything to erase the memory of his dramatic experience. In short, he was no person to perceive or understand the vagaries and conflicts of an inexperienced, confused, female soul. "Remember, the devil makes work for idle hands," was the limit of his advice to her.

One day the sister Doorkeeper announced that there was a gentleman to see Sister Consuelo. Preoccupied as she was by the problems of the hospital, the news took her aback. She asked who it was, and the sister told her it was Augusto Aixelà's estate manager. Being born in the region, the Doorkeeper knew the man well. She told Sister Consuelo that the manager was called Pepet Bonaire and that, like Pudenciana, to whom he was related, he was as bald as a coot. He was very popular in the hospital, not only because he was a friendly, open sort of fellow but also because, as manager to the Aixelà family, it was he who personally brought the donations and gifts they bestowed on the institution. Sister Consuelo found him sitting on a bench in the entrance: he was a small, plumpish man, with slow gestures and an intelligent, wily look on his face. Although he was thought to be well on in years, since he had also managed the Aixelà de Collbató estate in the days of the present incumbent's father, he stood up with surprising agility as soon as he saw the Mother Superior, and bowed deeply to her. Despite the continuing heat, he was wearing a corduroy suit, a sash round his waist, and a peaked cap. He also wore a pair of high boots that were spattered with mud from the flooded fields. When Sister Consuelo asked him to come into her office, he replied that he had no wish to stay any longer than was strictly necessary. In fact, he explained, he had only come to return the file Don Augusto had given him. "Well, in that case, I won't hear of you leaving before you tell me what you think," Sister Consuelo insisted. "Step into my office and I'll have them bring you coffee and some fritters; the coffee is dishwater, but the fritters are made here in the convent and are supposed to be good – you've probably tried them before." "Yes, I have, and they're delicious, but I wouldn't want to put you to any trouble; I've heard you've had lots of problems with the recent floods, and that you've closed down the operating theatre." As the estate manager was saying this, the Mother Superior gently led him to her office: he did not resist. Once installed, they spent some time talking about her proposed budget, but Sister Consuelo could scarcely pay any attention to what the man was saying: he was a practical, extremely meticulous person, and in the Mother Superior's view lost himself in a wealth of detail which, although important, seemed to her to be of little real relevance. If I carry on listening to him, I'll lose all interest in the project, she thought to herself. She struggled silently to find a way to change the topic of their conversation without offending him. Finally she succeeded in bringing the talk round to Augusto Aixelà's dealings in Madrid. "It was really generous and praiseworthy of him to have spent time on my little project, taking him from his own business," Sister Consuelo said, and when the manager simply nodded in agreement, she added, "especially considering how important it is." "As you say, reverend mother," the estate manager said. "Don José," said the nun, not daring to call him Pepet, much less to use the nickname he was known by locally, "don't think me indiscreet, but I know nothing about Señor Aixelà's business in Madrid. I am aware it concerns the Ministry of the Interior and that it is extremely important; I have no wish to pry into anyone's life, and if it is something personal please do not tell me anything about it, but if as I suspect it is something more than that, and I can help in some way to resolve or simply mitigate it, please don't hesitate to tell me what it involves." The estate manager smiled, fell serious, then another fleeting smile crossed his features, as though he were debating the matter in his head. Finally he looked up at the nun once more, settled back in his seat and pushed his legs out in front of him. He folded his hands across his stomach and said: "I don't see what you could do in this case, but on the other hand one never knows; at any rate, since it is no secret, I can't see any reason not to tell you; after all, you are the Mother Superior here at the hospital, and therefore a prominent person in the region." He leaned forward slightly and said: "A little less than a year ago, a bandit appeared in the hills. Even though there had been no bandits round here since the end of the war, no-one was particularly worried: there have always been bandits in the hills, just as there are pickpockets in the cities. In general," he went on, "they are not bad people. They live from day to day, and only need to show a bit of courage and imagination for people to take to them: after all, there is not much entertainment around here, and when it comes down to it, nobody is that fond of authority." The old man adopted the unhurried tone of someone about to launch into a long story, and began: "When I was a boy, my father, may he rest in peace, used to tell me about a bandit in these mountains who was called Antonio Llobet, although he was better known as Tiarrú, because he was a fine figure of a man, swaggering like a peacock. Until he was killed in a shoot-out with the Civil Guard, he came to the village fair every year: he would dance with all the women, he didn't care whether they were pretty or ugly, he grabbed them all. Then after the dancing he would go into the inn and order wine for everyone, going from table to table making toasts. And when I was a bit older, I can remember one called Juan Budallés, alias Mierdafrita, who had quite a reputation: he would turn up at the bullfights whenever they held them in Bassora, and it was he who decided whether a matador should receive one bull's ear or two, or on the contrary should be grabbed and tossed in the river; and whatever he said went, even if the Minister of the Interior himself was present. One day when this bandit went to a house to ask for some food, as he often did, the man of the house said he was going to the pantry to get it, but instead locked the door and ran off, without thinking that he was leaving his wife and children behind. He had barely gone half a mile when he met up with a couple of Civil Guardsmen on horseback. 'Hurry up,' he told them, 'Mierdafrita is locked in my house.' But when he saw the two men galloping towards him, the bandit shot the lock away and just managed to escape: he had not wanted to stay holed up in the house because the woman and children might have been hurt in the shooting. That Sunday, when the whole village came out of Mass, they found Budallés and his gang waiting outside the church. The man who had betrayed him gave himself up for dead, but his wife reacted more swiftly: she went down on her knees in front of the bandit and begged him: 'Don't kill my man, Mierdafrita.' 'I won't kill him, woman,' said the bandit, 'but I have to teach him a lesson so that he learns to keep his mouth shut.' Then he turned to the informer and ordered: 'Take your trousers down, you louse.' Don't worry, sister, it was allright in the end: he took his revenge with a few lashes of the whip. The authorities did not show him the same mercy when they finally laid hands on him: they garroted him in the yard at Bassora jail in the same year that our century began, which some say was in 1900, and others 1901." The nun's dismay at hearing all these savage tales was matched by the old man's relish as he warmed to the telling of them. "I could spend the whole afternoon telling you more stories, sister: as I said, there have always been bandits hereabouts, and each and every one of them had his name and his legend: Pedro el Torrat, Niseto el de la Bomba, Saltatrenes, Luisito el Gafas; there was even Saturnino, who they reckon was a woman who became an outlaw after she had been raped by the militia; but to cut a long story short, it's as I said: they were decent people who did not cause trouble if they were left alone to live their lives." He paused for a while, then frowned and went on: "And yet, this time around, for no apparent reason, Don Augusto got very nervous: he started saying that the bandit was the leader of a large gang and was planning to kidnap him; on other occasions he denied there was any such bandit, but said it was a group of Republican maquis who were out to settle scores for things that had happened during the war. There may have been some truth on both counts: there has been more than one kidnapping, and there are many wounds from the war that have not yet healed. In any case, Don Augusto kept on at the Civil Guard to go out into the hills and deal with the danger he imagined to be there; then later, when the searches the Civil Guard made brought no result, he went to Barcelona to ask the military governor to have the army intervene. The military governor refused point blank: the government has never wanted the army mixed up in these matters, even in the worst years of the maquis. So Don Augusto took himself to Madrid, where he must have been doing the rounds, wheedling and insisting, Heaven knows with what success. That is what he has told me, at least. If in fact he went to Madrid for other purposes, I could not say; and now I must go." "Do you really think that Don Augusto's life is in danger?" the Mother Superior asked. The estate manager shrugged his shoulders and raised his eyes to the ceiling. "What will be, will be," he said. Sister Consuelo did not like to insist, because she was unsure whether the man was as simple-minded as his reply suggested or whether, as seemed more likely, he preferred to leave things in the air. "He must know something he isn't telling me," she thought. When she was alone again in her cell, the figures of the bandits, who had seemed picturesque inventions when the estate manager had spoken of them, now appeared to her as frighteningly real: she imagined them, hirsute and grim-faced, about to wield an axe above the defenceless, crumpled figure of Augusto Aixelà. This fantasy, born of her fears, seemed to her the premonition of something that was bound to happen, and it plunged her into despair as though it were taking place there and then.

4

THE CIVIL Guard post was in a street that led down to the river from the church square. It was a whitewashed two-storey building, only identifiable by the Spanish flag crudely painted on the wall above the entrance, together with the well-known slogan: EVERYTHING FOR THE FATHERLAND. A skinny dog covered in flies slumbered on the pavement outside the doorway. The Mother Superior and the convent Bursar peered cautiously inside: the room was dominated by a large table on which stood a black fan with tin blades, humming noisily. A Civil Guardsman, with a moustache and a fat paunch, sat at the table. It seemed he was not expecting any visitors in such a scorching time of the afternoon, because he was in his undershirt and was apparently absorbed in reading an El Coyote thriller. On the floor next to the table stood an earthenware jug; the man's jacket and three-cornered hat hung from a hanger, and his shotgun was propped up in the angle of the two far walls. Confronted with this stark spectacle, with one mind the two nuns beat a hasty retreat. "What did we come for?" the bursar asked as they scurried back down the street. "Oh, nothing, nothing," the Mother Superior replied. Their presence had not gone unnoticed by the Civil Guardsman: by now he was standing in the doorway buttoning up his jacket, unaware that his braces hung down on either side. He stared dumbfounded at the two women running away, at a loss as to why they should have wanted to disturb his siesta in this way.

When they reached the entrance to the convent, the sister Doorkeeper came out to greet them with the news that there was another visitor. "It's Señor Aixelà!" she muttered, grimacing with emotion. The Mother Superior smiled: the presence of such a smart, rich gentleman had visibly affected the nun. "I took the liberty of showing him into your office," the other woman said. "It did not seem right to keep him waiting out in the hall. Especially considering all he has done for us!" "You were quite right, sister," said the Mother Superior soothingly then, turning to the bursar: "Get on with your work, Mother Millas, I'll send for you if necessary." A shadow flitted across the Bursar's features. She's jealous, Sister Consuelo thought, then corrected herself: Who am I to judge – what do I know of these things after all? She strode off to her office, and flung open the door. Augusto Aixelà started from his seat. "Goodness gracious, what's the matter?" he asked. The Mother Superior came in and shut the door behind her. "Nothing," she replied. "I thought you had come determined to see me off the premises," he said. "Not at all. I was told there was someone waiting for me, so I hurried in: I don't like to keep people waiting." "I haven't been here long, and this time it was I who came without any warning," he replied. "I thought that with this heat you were bound to be indoors, but I see you're not daunted by high temperatures." "A short while ago we had a serious problem with the operating theatre because of the floods, and I wanted to send letters reporting it, as is my duty, to the proper authorities and to the Provincial Superior. I decided it would be best to go to the post office at this quiet time of day," she said, then sighed, fell silent for a while, and added in a calmer voice: "I must admit though that this heat is bothersome; excuse me, will you?" She went over to a pine dresser standing against the wall, which had a china jug and basin on it. She poured water into the basin, washed her hands and

44

face, then dried herself with a damp, threadbare towel that was hanging from a nail beside the dresser. While she was doing this, she became aware of the disgusting smell of boiled cabbage clinging to her habit, which even the walk in the fresh air had not managed to dispel. "Don't you have running water?" Augusto Aixelà asked behind her back. "We do in the hospital," the nun replied, "but not in our residence." As she spoke, she opened the window, picked up the washbasin, and tossed the dirty water out. "The river is still running high," she commented. "Reverend mother," her visitor butted in, "would you mind closing the window, leaving the basin where it belongs, and paying me some attention?" "Oh, I'm so sorry," she said, mortified. "I came to talk about your project: don't tell me you've lost interest in it already." "No, no, on the contrary," she protested, "what on earth makes you think that?" "It's only human nature to weaken just when our dreams are about to come true," said Augusto Aixelà. Sister Consuelo's features hardened: "I don't play games," she said firmly. "I know," he replied, "and I also know you've been talking to Pepet." The nun responded: "Your manager was kind enough to come and visit me. We looked at the project closely together, and he made some very valuable comments about it." "He has a lot of experience," Augusto Aixelà said: "he's getting on a bit, and with the years he's become rather grumpy and irritable, but he knows everyone around here, and they all like and respect him. If your project gets off the ground, his help will be essential." "I'm counting on it," the nun said, "but might I ask what brings you here?" "I would be lying if I said there was a precise reason, at least as far as your project is concerned," he replied: "I still have no news from Madrid." His gaze wandered around the walls of the room for a moment, then he added: "I heard about the flood and the closure of your operating theatre, so I thought I ought to come and find out what had happened: ever since you got me involved in the hospital, I've felt personally responsible for it." "If it was me who imposed that burden on you, and not your own conscience, I absolve you from it here and now," Sister Consuelo said in the same bantering fashion. "But in any case, I thank you for your interest." "Don't thank me for that," Augusto Aixelà said. "I also came because I missed your company and your conversation." "There must be precious little to do in this village if you can miss the gossip of a poor, ignorant nun," the Mother Superior replied. "Don't be such a hypocrite, or you'll be banished headlong to hell," he retorted, "and remember, you promised you would come and see my art collection." "I made no such promise, and you know very well I cannot do so," Sister Consuelo replied, a trace of sadness in her voice. "On the contrary," he came back: "I think that you not only can, but you should. The works of art in my collection are all religious; there is nothing profane about them. To me, it is just art, but to you they could be not only beautiful but edifying; in the same way that being close to a virtuous, open-minded person is bound to be for me." "Are you referring to me?" the nun asked, slightly at a loss: she had no idea how to take such an odd line of reasoning. He stared at her. "Have you never thought that Providence had some reason for making our paths cross?" he asked. "Sometimes I wonder who it really was who did so," the nun muttered. "So, you'll come then?" he pressed her, then added, before she could say anything: "Bring the Bursar with you if you wish."

The dogs ran barking towards her, but when they reached her side, they sniffed at her habit and fell quiet. Sister Consuelo still preferred not to move until Pudenciana arrived. "They must have recognised you," the housekeeper said. "Yes," the nun replied, "sometimes my habit smells of ether, at others of cabbage or of soap, but they still always recognise the person wearing it: I wonder how they do it?" "They're smarter than we are in some things," the housekeeper declared: "sometimes I reckon they can even sniff out who is coming here with good or with bad intentions." Sister Consuelo timidly stretched out her hand towards one of the dogs, and when she saw it did not react in a hostile manner, began to stroke its massive head. "Don't take it too far, woman," the house-keeper said. As the two of them walked towards the house they met the gardener. He was carrying a hosepipe rolled up over one shoulder, and the metal nozzle hanging down behind him traced a curved furrow in the earth. As the nun passed by him, he gazed at her open-mouthed. "Close your mouth, you dope, before you swallow a fly," Pudenciana said to him. "He was very kind to me the other day," the nun said, "he accompanied me to the gate and protected me from the dogs." "Ha; he hasn't the faintest idea of anything he does," Pudenciana snorted: "when he was a child he got the fever, and that was that: he can't understand or think prop-erly." Sister Consuelo stared into the gardener's eyes and saw their impenetrable emptiness. She shuddered, and the two women continued on their way down to the house. "Did the master ask you to come at this time?" the housekeeper asked when they were in the hall. "He asked me to come, but not at this precise moment," the nun replied: "in fact, he said I should come to see him without specifying any particular time, or day for that matter: is it wrong of me?" "Oh, no, you can come whenever you like, sister; and would that your presence here can be a good influence. But the master went out hunting this morning and he's resting right now: as you know, they have to get up before dawn for their hunting trips. But I'll go and call him anyway." "No, don't do that, let him sleep – I'll come back another day," the nun said hastily. Then all

47

of a sudden she collapsed into one of the wicker chairs and announced, in flat contradiction to what she had just said: "I'll wait here until he gets up." Pudenciana scratched her head in bewilderment. "I'll go and see to your lemonade," she said eventually. "No, don't worry, I'm not thirsty: what did you mean when you said that I might be able to exert a good influence here?" Sister Consuelo wanted to know. Pudenciana scratched her head once more. "The master needs a kindly soul to set him back on the straight and narrow," she declared. "Why, has he strayed so far from it?" the nun asked. The housekeeper gave a knowing smile that belied the seriousness of her tone. "Ah, sister, if only the walls could talk!" she sighed. The Mother Superior stood up. "The walls cannot talk, Pudenciana, but you can," she said, "and if you have any respect for the crucifix hanging from my waist, in its name I call upon you to tell me all you know." The housekeeper was stunned by the fierceness of this exhortation. "Good God," she muttered, "don't pay any mind to what I say: I'm only a simple villager, what would I know about anything?" "Don't play the innocent," the nun retorted, "I've been looking after the sick for twenty years now, and I have thirteen nuns who work under me, so I know all the excuses and tricks a human mind can invent." At this, the housekeeper brought a chair over next to the one the nun had been sitting in until a moment earlier, and they both sat down. "The problem is women," Pudenciana said slowly, as if she were embarking on the explanation of a difficult theory, "they are his downfall. You wouldn't think it to look at him, he's so serious and formal, but still waters run deep, as the saying goes. When he was young," she went on, "he had the devil in his flesh, and now he's older he hasn't changed a whit – and that's not good, sister, it's not good either for the health or the pocket, or the eternal salvation of the soul, though I hate to say it. Of course, all men are born rogues, but the master has caused a lot of hurt, and those who go fishing in other people's ponds must expect resentment and violence." All of a sudden, Pudenciana stood up and declared: "I belong to this house, and won't say anything more." Before she could leave the room – if that had been her intention – Sister Consuelo got up quickly and took her by the arm. The two women began to walk up and down the hall, with their heads close together; their whispering floated off into the darkness of the bare room. "Wasn't there ever a woman who could make him settle down?" "Years ago," the housekeeper replied, "many years ago. There was one woman who loved him a lot; not like the others, who simply wanted a good time and a bit of fun, if you'll pardon me saying so, then goodbye, I'll be seeing you . . . no, this one was serious, but it didn't work out. She must have thought she could forgive him his faults because she loved him so much, and take him as he was, or even get him to change his ways, but she didn't succeed." "Why? What happened?" "How should I know?" the housekeeper complained: "I spend all day going from the henhouse to the stove, how would I know what goes on? It's said he tormented her so much that in the end she lost her mind: ah, if only these walls could talk! One fine day we no longer saw her here, she left and never came back. Some time later, there was a rumour she had died a horrible death: that's all I know." The housekeeper fell silent, as if the memory of the other person's misfortune weighed on her conscience. "I was very young too in those days," she went on somewhat illogically, "it was just after the Civil War. The master had entered the village at the head of the Franco forces; his father, who was still alive then, had spent the whole of the war in safety in France; but the master had spurned that security, crossed through the lines, and went to fight for his own side. He wore a pistol stuck in his belt, and you should have seen how well the Falange uniform suited him: all the girls sighed for him, the unmarried ones and the married ones too – perhaps even more." The nun stopped short and let go of the housekeeper's arm. "I know nothing about that kind of thing," she said sharply, "why are you telling me such nonsense?" Pudenciana lowered her eyes, afraid she had overstepped the mark. "You can do a lot for him, I'm sure," she stammered. "I can see from your face that you are a saint; you have the look of a saint."

At this point, Augusto Aixelà's entrance cut short their conversation. "What are you gossiping about, Pudenciana?" he growled. The housekeeper stifled a shriek of alarm. Augusto Aixelà was wearing a silk dressing gown, under which could be seen the legs of a striped pair of pyjamas. It was the contained anger in his look which so frightened Pudenciana. "I was keeping the sister here company," the housekeeper stammered. She was trembling with fear. Sister Consuelo took her by the arm again and smiled as if to say: Don't worry, I'm not going to repeat a single word of what you've told me. "A lot of chitchat, but you haven't even brought her a glass of water: what will she think of our hospitality?" the landowner scolded her; "and why didn't you tell me she was here?" "She wanted to, but I wouldn't have it," the nun retorted, "when I heard that you had been hunting." "That's right, but don't tell anyone; it's not the season yet. You can leave now, Pudenciana, but don't stray too far, in case we need you," he went on, still looking at the nun, "and please forgive me for the way we received you, I had gone to lie down for a while. Please go into my study, I'll get dressed and be with you at once."

As soon as the housekeeper had withdrawn, but before Augusto Aixelà had found time to do so, the mother superior whispered hastily: "I could not come accompanied as you suggested because there is a lot of work at the hospital." "In that case," the landowner said before he closed the study door behind him, "I'm doubly grateful for your visit." Left on her own in the room, the nun began to pace up and down in a highly nervous fashion. Why did I come here; what am I doing here? she asked herself. There's no point trying to find excuses: God can see all I do – yes, but does he understand me? This thought, which seemed to have been formulated independently of her will, made her come to a halt in a state of panic. What am I saying? I must really have gone mad to think such a thing; what's wrong with me? She peered round the room, as though the mutilated statues might supply her with the answer to her doubts. Then she saw an antique mirror hanging from one of the walls; accustomed as she was to the austerity of life in the convent, the reflection of her own image seemed strange to her, and her curiosity made her approach the mirror. She could barely recognise the face in the speckled glass: the eyes stared out with a strange, intense gleam. The darkness of the study lent the mirror an air of bottomless depth, in which this fraught face was floating. I'm suffocating, she thought: I need air or I'll faint. She tried to open the door which led onto the veranda, but found she could not shift the bolt: she had neither the strength nor the skill to make her hands comply. Breathless, she crossed the study and went out into the hall; the two chairs where she and the housekeeper had exchanged secrets and confidences were still next to each other, breaking up the austere symmetry of the other furniture. The nun strode across the hall, opened the door through which Pudenciana had fled in order to escape her master's wrath, and went into a darkened room. She was overwhelmed by a repulsive smell that was very familiar to her, but which she found hard to imagine in this house. She groped along a wall until she found a switch, turned it on, and a naked bulb hanging from the ceiling on a flex lit up the room. She could now see she was in a kind of larder, one of whose walls was filled by a dresser where earthenware jars were stored; on the opposite wall, a couple of dozen hooks hung from a metal rod; the same number of freshly killed rabbits dangled from them, dripping blood. The corpses seemed to be staring down at the nun with a crazed expression to which fear had lent an extraordinary ferocity. The blood dripping from this doleful cluster fell into an aluminium bucket with an irregular, plopping sound. Filled with pity and disgust at such a sight, the nun turned on her heel, intending to head back into the hall, but as she did so, she bumped into Augusto Aixelà, who had come into the room behind her without her noticing it. She stifled a scream of shock, her body convulsed and then slumped weakly. "Don't be frightened," he said, taking her by the shoulders to calm her down: "they're only dead rabbits." "How did you get in?" the nun asked, in the faintest of voices. "Through the door, like you. Are you sure your wimple doesn't affect your hearing? It's the second time this has happened." "That must have something to do with it," Sister Consuelo said, recovering her composure and removing the landowner's hands from her shoulders. "I'll make sure I come to see you whenever I have the hiccoughs." Then she added, with a frown: "Are these what you killed this morning?" Augusto Aixelà did not notice the reproachful look in the nun's eyes, and answered: "There have been better days, but I can't complain." He looked up proudly at the dead rabbits and added: "I'll have some of them wrapped up for you so that you can take them to the hospital: I wouldn't know what to do with so much meat." "I thank you for the gift in the name of the hospital," the nun said, "but if you had no need of the meat, why did you kill them?" "For sport," Augusto Aixelà said in a surprised tone, "for years now hunting has been a pastime rather than a way to get food, and as such it's to be enjoyed for its own sake. Don't tell me that's news to you." "No, but I don't understand what pleasure there can possibly be in the act of killing a living creature." "Are you always going to be scolding me?" he protested: "that's what rabbits are for, isn't it? If we didn't kill them, they would take over the fields and destroy everything: you know how quickly they breed, and how greedy and destructive they are. Besides, what's wrong with killing animals? The apostles were fishermen, and when all is said and done, death is ordained by God as well." "He does not ordain it, he tolerates it, and that is very different." Augusto Aixelà burst out laughing. "What if we continue our theological discussion somewhere more pleasant?" Sister Consuelo nodded: she was ashamed for having started the argument. Hunting did not offend her conscience: as a girl, she had seen her father and brothers coming home from the fields with their double-barrelled shotguns, their knapsacks stuffed with hares and partridges. In those days she herself had helped by setting traps and laying birdlime to catch thrushes and larks which ended up fried on the dinner table. I was only annoyed because of the shock he gave me, she reasoned: my nervous system is upset, and I can't control my reactions. A while ago in the study I was hysterical, now in this ghastly place I'm perfectly calm, I can even joke or give moral discourses. Oh, there's no point in lying to myself: the change is because he's here — but how can I feel so safe standing next to him after all the dreadful things Pudenciana was telling me? Bah, those ghastly stories must be lies; if they weren't, I wouldn't feel so secure.

5

THEY LEFT the hall again, but this time went up a staircase to the top floor of the house. They walked down a long, wide corridor whose walls were hung with enormous portraits. Tiny specks of dust could be seen floating in the air where streaks of light shone through chinks in the curtains shielding the paintings from the sunlight. The portraits were solemn and lacking in expression, but their sheer size and the varied dress of the subjects made them look imposing. From all of them, even those of children who had doubtless died of measles or whooping cough in the first flush of life, there emanated a sense of absurdity that made them somehow unappealing. Augusto Aixelà made no attempt to inform his guest about the paintings or who they might depict. The corridor led into a circular room with a high, vaulted ceiling. Its walls were hung with silk, and the ceiling was decorated with chaste allegorical figures who held bunches of flowers and fruits in their plump arms. Silverware shone from chests, showcases, ornate cabinets; the stiff polychrome of porcelain glowed in the warm afternoon light. But they did not come to a halt here either.

They went on instead into a bedroom which smelt of camphor, furnished with monastic frugality. The fourposter bed was made up, as though it were in regular use, and on the desk was a vase of wild flowers. Before Sister Consuelo could express her surprise, Augusto Aixelà said: "This was my mother's bedroom. She spent the long years of her illness here, and it was here that she died. First my father then I myself have kept the room just as she left it; we keep it cleaned and with fresh bedlinen, but nobody has used it since that sad day. Occasionally," he said, lowering his voice, "I come here on my own for a while. I sit in this chair, where she liked to watch the hours go by, staring out of the window . . . I took the liberty of bringing you here because I wanted you to see it; I have never shown it to anyone before." Sister Consuelo went over to the window and drew back the cretonne curtains. She looked out at the garden and the pond in the distance, then let the curtains drop, and leant against the edge of the desk. Augusto Aixelà took her arm. "You've gone pale. Don't you feel well?" In response, she let herself be led quietly down the stairs and out of the house until they were on the veranda. The parrot greeted her with shrill, metallic screeches. Evening was drawing in.

"Sit down, I'll have you brought something to drink," he said. "No, don't go to any trouble . . . and above all, don't go," the nun begged him, "the calm here will do me more good than anything else, I'll be perfectly all right if I can just sit here for a while." She closed her eyes and sat motionless; her face was still pallid, and her heart was beating as though she had just made an exhausting effort. She sat quite still. Augusto Aixelà watched her without saying a word. Unannounced, Pudenciana arrived with a glass of cold water. The landowner took the glass and motioned for the housekeeper to leave them. Then he placed his free hand on the nun's cheek. It was feverish. When she felt the touch of his fingers, she opened her eyes and looked at him with an expression of profound sadness. "Drink this water," he said, offering her the glass. She drank it all in tiny sips, then stood up and for no apparent reason walked away from the veranda, as if her action was in response to a call. Augusto

Aixelà remained in his seat: he saw her first cross the garden, then disappear beneath the arch of trimmed cypresses that led to the vegetable patch. At that, he got up and followed her, walking deliberately slowly. When he reached the vegetable garden, he stopped and looked again: the nun was wandering along the footpath between the rows of plants, lost in her thoughts. Realizing she did not wish to be disturbed, he stayed where he was without doing anything to draw attention to himself. All of a sudden, there was a peal of thunder; when he looked up, he could see storm clouds sweeping across the sky. He caught up with Sister Consuelo by the pond and said to her: "It's going to rain, we'd better go inside," but she did not hear a word: leaning over the sluice, she was staring fascinated at the mass of churning water. "Don't go too close," Augusto Aixelà warned her as he came alongside, "this pond is treacherous. The water is much deeper than it looks, and the edges aren't safe because of the mud. There's a legend that a young girl drowned here once when she was cheated in love, and ever since then, so the story goes, the pond has been cursed." The nun crossed herself, but did not take her eyes from the water. By now the clouds had completely covered the sky, and turned the surface of the water black. For a brief moment, their shadow created vague shapes in the water that seemed to spring from the depths of the pond, but before these images could take on any proper form, heavy raindrops began to fall in dense circles on the water. The drops became a downpour. Seeing that the nun still stood rooted to the spot, without reacting to the rain, Augusto Aixelà took her by the shoulders and made her turn round. "Hurry, or we'll get drenched," he shouted, struggling to make himself heard above the noise of the storm. They both started to run through the muddy garden towards the house. Swept by the wind, the sheeting rain made it hard to make out the blurred outline of the arch of cypresses.

Augusto Aixelà still held on firmly to Sister Consuelo, as though to prevent her being blown away by the gusts of wind that whipped the tree branches and bent the tomato canes double. She let herself be almost carried along, as docile and weak as though her naturally tough physique had given way just as her state of mind had. When they reached the veranda they stopped, but for a few seconds were still entwined. The parrot was squawking with fright; Augusto Aixelà brought his lips close to the nun's mouth, but she gently pushed him away. "No," she said in a whisper. She wriggled free of his grasp, rushed to the door leading to his study, and went in. Augusto Aixelà followed her: inside, a surprise awaited them.

Standing in the centre of the study, the Civil Guard sergeant was staring curiously at the sight of this odd, dishevelled couple. He was wearing his cape and hat, but had left his shotgun propped against the wall. "Goodness gracious, what are you doing here, Lastre?" the landowner exclaimed, and before the other had the chance to reply, he added: "We were caught by the storm out in the garden, and we're soaking wet." He spoke with such haste and confusion that the sergeant could not help but notice. Both Augusto Aixelà and Sister Consuelo were wondering whether he had witnessed the scene out on the veranda. "I don't think you two know each other," the master of the house went on, by now his usual composed self: "Sergeant Lastre here has the task of keeping the peace and ensuring order in the region – something that's not always easy. Sister Consuelo is the director of the hospital." The sergeant lifted his hand to his hat, but paused just as he was about to give a military salute, hesitated and finally decided it would be more appropriate to take his hat off to the nun. She for her part had bent her head in greeting, and missed his ceremonial indecisiveness as the damp ends of her wimple flapped across her face.

"Have we not met before, sister?" asked the sergeant. The nun recalled the abortive visit to the Civil Guard post with the convent bursar, but refrained from mentioning it. "Perhaps we've passed each other in the street," she said, in such a studiously bashful tone that the landowner had to smile. They're all exactly the same, he thought, then, turning to the Civil Guardsman: "I'm sorry not to be able to attend to you as I would wish, but it is urgent that Sister Consuelo gets back to the hospital as quickly as possible if we don't want her to catch pneumonia." The sergeant interpreted this disguised command correctly and said: "I'll take care of it: if you will allow me, I'll accompany her back to the hospital myself. I purposely came in the Land Rover, thinking it might rain as it has done; with the ground so slippery, she will be safer with me. The weather forecast," the sergeant continued, "warned there would be a storm, and the authorities have taken every precaution to ensure that nothing like what happened recently in Bassora and elsewhere in Catalonia should take place again. People are very worried though," he added. "As for my business here, it is neither pressing nor extremely important; I'll perhaps call by tomorrow, Don Augusto, unless you would prefer to drop in at the post." "You come, Lastre," the landowner replied, "if the weather and your duties permit it. We can taste a smoked ham that I've just received, which is crying out to be eaten." The sergeant put his hat back on and saluted. He stepped to one side to allow Augusto Aixelà to open the door; the nun went out into the hall without once lifting her eyes from the floor, and the two men followed her. It was still pouring with rain outside. "I'll bring the jeep up to the door," the sergeant said, wrapping himself in his cape, the gun-metal blue of his shotgun poking through its folds. Taking advantage of the disappearance of this inopportune witness, Augusto Aixelà grasped the nun's frozen hand and pulled her towards him. "Come

58

back tomorrow," he said. She withdrew her hand and shook her head. "At least look me in the face," he protested, but all she did was repeat the same gesture. By now the jeep had drawn up in front of the house. "Won't you change your mind?" pleaded Augusto Aixelà. Sister Consuelo raised her head and stared at him with a look bordering on the insane. "Not even in death," she cried, and ran out to the vehicle. The sergeant opened the door, which boasted in its centre the shield of the glorious Civil Guard; as soon as she had got in, he shut it, circled the jeep and climbed in behind the steering wheel. They had already begun to drive off when Pudenciana came running out of the house, carrying a large package wrapped in a chequered cloth. She hopped between the puddles and handed it to Sister Consuelo through the Land Rover window. The mud from the jeep's rear wheels spattered the house-keeper's apron from top to bottom. When they had passed through the gate and out onto the road, the nun untied the cloth to see what was inside: several dead rabbits slithered to the floor of the jeep.

Buffeted by the jolting vehicle, which bounced over the roughest parts of the track, forded rushing torrents of water, and generally made its way across country through the sheeting rain, Sister Consuelo groped to pick up the rabbits which were rolling all over the floor. More concerned about his driving than his companion, the sergeant asked her what she was doing, what she was looking for underneath the seats. The nun replied with an unintelligible mutter. The sergeant slowed down. "I know they are rabbits," he said, raising his gruff voice above the noise of the engine and the clanging of the bodywork, "and I also know Don Augusto hunts them out of season, but it's all the same to me: after all, it's his land, they're his rabbits, and poaching is none of my business anyway. I'm more worried about the way he goes out into the hills at times like these; I've told him a thousand times that one of these days he will end up like one of those blasted rabbits, if you'll excuse the expression." The nun had managed to tie up her bundle again, and sat back in her seat. I must look a sight, she thought to herself. She said to the sergeant: "So it's true that the mountains are dangerous?" The Civil Guardsman gave a sharp tug on the wheel which almost resulted in them turning over: "Would I be here if they weren't?" he roared. As the question seemed to imply what the answer must be, the nun said nothing.

In her cell, she dried herself and changed her clothes, then hastened to the refectory, where the whole community, apart from those who were looking after the sick, were waiting for her to say grace. She made a superhuman effort to eat, partly because it did not seem right to turn her nose up at a breast of chicken with peppers while the rest of the nuns were avidly devouring their watery gruel, and partly because she could see that the Bursar was surreptitiously observing her. Mother Millas had been the convent Bursar for many years, and at the same time dealt with all the hospital's complicated financial affairs. She carried out both functions disastrously, being extremely incompetent and disorganised; yet, despite this, no-one had doubted that on the retirement of the previous Mother Superior she would take over as a reward for her years of service and devotion. However, when the occasion arose, the Provincial Superior – judging perhaps that Mother Millas was not only inefficient in her work, but was also a somewhat difficult person, whose ineptness in her social relations was a constant source of misunderstandings and problems with the other nuns, the patients, the convent suppliers, in fact, with everyone who came into contact with her – decided to pass her over and appoint Sister Consuelo instead. Although much younger than Mother

Millas, the Provincial Superior and her Board felt that Sister Consuelo was much better suited to the task. Since the new Mother Superior and the Bursar would have to work closely together, the Provincial Superior left it up to Sister Consuelo to decide whether she would confirm Mother Millas in her post as Bursar, or choose someone new. Naturally Sister Consuelo swiftly confirmed Mother Millas in her old job, asserting that nobody could do it better, and adding that she was sure that the relation between the two of them would be easy, pleasant and beneficial to both. Since then there had been no reason for her to complain about the way they worked together, but it was only logical to suppose that Mother Millas, perhaps without herself being fully aware of it, should harbour some resentment for the string of humiliations she had been made to suffer. Try as she might to pretend she did not notice how she was being scrutinised, Sister Consuelo found it impossible to eat: the mere idea of swallowing a piece of chicken made her feel ill. Once dinner was over, she used the excuse of feeling tired to substitute the reading of some fragments from a book of pious meditations for her usual edifying talk to her flock. She was secretly hoping that the storm would distract the nuns so that they would not pay her too much attention, because she had not the faintest idea of what she was reading, did not understand the phrases she was saying, and was not even sure that she was uttering comprehensible sounds. By now the Bursar was staring at her with a frightening intensity. Sister Consuelo felt a lump in her throat which made it impossible for her to go on reading. I can't burst into tears in front of all the nuns, she thought, and signalled for Mother Millas to come up and take her place at the lectern. "Getting wet this afternoon must have given me a cold," she said. "I don't feel well; you read, Mother Millas if you would, and I'll listen." The Bursar began in a dull monotone:

"Those who truly love, love all that is good, wish for all that is good, favour all that is good, praise all that is good; they love only things that are true and noble; they do not enter into conflicts or feel jealousy, because their only desire is to satisfy the loved one; they are ready to die for his love, and devote their lives to discovering how they can better please him." When Mother Millas had reached this point, Sister Consuelo let out such a loud sob that she was obliged to break off her reading. In a hushed silence, the Mother Superior took a handkerchief out of her habit sleeve and blew her nose, fervently hoping that this desperate cry from the depths of her soul would be mistaken for a sneeze. Then she said: "Go on if you please, Mother Millas."

The storm continued until late into the night. Cruel flashes of lightning sneaked through the shutters of Sister Consuelo's cell and filled its walls with fleeting phantoms. The claps of thunder sounded like the crack of doom, they seemed to come from beyond the grave, and thunderbolts striking the ground left a smell of sulphur in the air. For the first time in her life, Sister Consuelo felt the terror of divine wrath, and spent endless hours with her head buried under the bedclothes, imploring the Blessed Virgin Mary's aid. As the night progressed she was led to think long and hard about what had happened the previous afternoon, and in general on the events which had led up to her present situation, which she realised was completely untenable. She vowed in the sternest terms to make good the harm she had done, and to close the door to any fresh occasion for sin. With the first light of dawn she composed a long letter to the Provincial Superior. In it Sister Consuelo confessed all her mistakes down to the last detail: "I set my eye and my desires on a human object, and I have attempted to disguise my error through lies. A pride which I have no hesitation in describing as Satanic led me to believe that I could take on the world and emerge unscathed from my contact with it; I now realise how wrong I was, and how weak the human soul is faced with the torments of passion, if our most merciful God is not there to protect us with his divine grace." For these reasons, the letter went on, she begged forgiveness from the reverend Provincial Superior and through her from the Superior General. She placed herself in their hands, and was ready to receive whatever punishment they deemed fit to impose on her. For her part, she wished to renew her vows of obedience, poverty and chastity, and implored the authorities of her order to allow her to be transferred elsewhere, far from where she now was, and to change from the apostolic life and caring for the sick to a contemplative one of perpetual silence and solitude. She read over the whole letter, felt satisfied, and signed it. Then she put it in an envelope, addressed it to the Provincial Superior of her order, and put a stamp on the letter. After that she took another sheet of paper and began a second letter, addressed this time to Augusto Aixelà, in which she wrote the following: "Dear Sir, I find myself obliged for reasons of health to leave the hospital at once and transfer to another location; I should not however wish to leave without saying goodbye to you and to thank you for all your kindness, while at the same time begging you to forgive me for any trouble I may have caused you. I have no way of knowing whether this decision," she went on, "will cause you the same pain it is causing me, but you must understand, my love, that sometimes it is necessary to open one's eyes to the light and to close one's heart to feelings; will you be able, I wonder, to understand this and to forgive me? I beg you to, my love, my treasure, because your forgiveness means more to me than that of God himself." She had got this far when she realised how ridiculous she was being. She tore the letter into tiny pieces, got up and flung open the shutters of her cell. The sun was just coming out; all traces of cloud had disappeared. Interpreting this unexpected gift as a sign of absolution, she gave thanks to God, washed, and went to answer the call to Matins. As she passed through the hallway on her way to chapel she met the postman, who was just giving the sister Doorkeeper the day's mail. "You're up and about early," she said to him. "Yes, sister," he replied, "there was no delivery yesterday because of the storm, so today it's double the work. Thankfully though," he went on, "there was no flooding this time." Another sign, the Mother Superior thought. She took the letter for the Provincial Superior from her pocket and gave it to the postman, saying: "Here, take this letter, would you? It will save me having to go to the post office."

Father Pallares was dozing in the confessional. "Father, I have felt the temptation of the flesh," she whispered, "and I have committed the sins of recklessness and pride." "My daughter, Almighty God permits the devil to tempt us in order to test our faith; but we must not fall into temptation, as Our Lord Jesus Christ taught us when three times he rejected the Evil One's offers and flattering words; you must pray a lot, prayer is the best answer." "I am very confused, father, help me." "Keep your mind on your work, my daughter, remember that God has given you an important task on this earth; but remember too that your work should never lead you into vanity or take you away from God. Just as Christ refused to be king of this world, so we should understand that work is nothing more than a means of approaching Christ: it is worthy if it helps us achieve that goal, unworthy if it distances us from it; and we must never permit our work to bind us to the things of this earth." Driven to distraction by all she had suffered in the sleepless hours of the previous night, Sister Consuelo took these empty phrases for a model of wisdom. "Thank you father, I see everything clearly now," she muttered, kissing the stole that projected through the confessional curtains. She took communion, and felt an enormous sense of wellbeing, as if everything that had caused her such despair the day before had been wiped from her life and memory. She went to bed that night physically exhausted, and fell asleep at once.

She awoke shortly before dawn, oppressed by a thought which had apparently formed in her mind while she was asleep, and which now seemed to her axiomatic and inevitable. If my letter was sent yesterday morning, it will be in the Provincial Superior's hands today, she said to herself, and that means, given what it contains, she will take immediate measures to transfer me . . . and that means I will probably have to leave here forever within two or three days. In that case, I cannot go without giving Augusto Aixelà some explanation; what has happened is not his fault, after all; if he has taken liberties with me, it is only because I gave him the opportunity to do so, and when all is said and done, he has not taken any vows binding him to a blameless life. She went on with her reasoning: I owe him a great many favours, not on a personal level, but as the representative of a religious order to which I would be doing a great injury if I left now without saying anything to him. God only knows to what extent he has compromised his good name and his inheritance by offering himself as guarantee for my fantasies to the authorities in Madrid. It would be truly ignoble of me if, thinking only of my own spiritual welfare, I were to behave towards him in such a haughty, ungrateful manner. This idea obsessed her throughout the day. Each passing hour was taking with it her last chance to say farewell to Augusto Aixelà, and she could find no argument to counter the pain that this certainty caused her. It would be useless to write to him, she told herself: I have already tried that, with disastrous results. I have to go and see him, to tell him face to face how things stand between us. After lunch, without telling anyone, she left the hospital. She told the Doorkeeper she was going on an errand, and would not be long. The sister nodded silently, and when she had left, shut the convent door behind her.

6

S HE HURRIED along, all the time looking back and around to make sure nobody had seen her, because that was the last thing she wanted. She halted at every road junction and only ventured across when she was certain that she would not bump into anyone. As she went round one bend, she saw the Civil Guard jeep coming towards her; she quickly hid in the bushes by the side of the road, scratching her hands on the brambles. The jeep passed just a few yards from her hiding place, raising a cloud of dust that hung motionless in the hot afternoon air. She did not emerge again until the sound of the engine had died away completely, and only the chirping of the crickets disturbed the quiet of the fields. When she reached the open gate she could not help but remember, with a nostalgic tug, the first occasion on which she had visited the house that she was now seeing for the last time, and how she had met up with the guard dogs who now, unlike then, came bounding up joyfully to greet her. "León, Negrita, my old friends," she said, stroking both of them. The dogs licked the blood oozing from her scratched hands. Then Pudenciana came up and said: "I was expecting you. The master told me you would come; I said you wouldn't, but he said: 'Yes, she'll come, be ready to receive her, and bring her here.'" "I've come to say goodbye, Pudenciana," the nun sighed. Augusto Aixelà met her in the study. "Leave us, Pudenciana," he ordered. "No, bring me a glass of water, my throat is parched," Sister Consuelo said, in the peremptory manner of someone who is used to being obeyed. The housekeeper hesitated. "Do as the Mother Superior tells you," Augusto Aixelà said. No sooner had Pudenciana gone out than he flung himself on the nun. She struggled to free herself from his grasp. "Let me go," she stammered. He did, and she shied away to the far end of the room. "If you don't want me to hold you, why have you come?" he wanted to know. "To say goodbye. I've written a long letter to the Provincial Superior. I explained that I have to leave here, and I've asked to be allowed to join an enclosed order. My decision is final; I've already sent the letter." She paused for a moment, cleared her throat, then added in a calmer voice: "I wanted to tell you face to face." Augusto Aixelà was silent, as if he were mulling over what he had just heard, then he asked: "Why do you want to bury yourself alive?" "Because I love you," came her speedy reply. "I don't know when or how I came to fall in love with you, because whenever I try to think when it was, it seems to me it has always been so. I try to understand, and I can find no reason on earth why I should not love you." Then she added: "Perhaps you are surprised to hear me admitting such things with almost indecent haste, but bear in mind that I do so as someone who is openly admitting her blame, and that my daily practice of the sacrament of confession has freed me from any sense of shame at my unworthiness." "What is so shameful about love?" asked Augusto Aixelà. "I would not know about love in general," Sister Consuelo replied, "but mine contradicts the will of God, and that is more than enough." "It's not God's will, but your own," he retorted, "you were the one who decided love should play no part in your life when you entered religion; but now that love has forced itself back on you, what sense does it make to keep shunning it? You took the decision, and you can change it: we are free agents, and God cannot possibly demand that you do something which will lead not only to your unhappiness, but mine too: that is unnatural and inhuman." "God demands my surrender to him, at whatever cost," replied the nun. "I knew that when I took my vows, and I am just as sure of it now, so I beg you not to insist, because this conversation will lead nowhere, and is extremely painful to me." Pudenciana came in with the glass of water. She handed it to the nun, who drank it straight off and gave it back to her. The housekeeper left the room again quickly and without a word; even though the two had said nothing, she could tell that questions of the utmost urgency were being resolved. Her brief interruption served to lighten the charged emotional atmosphere somewhat.

"What about your project?" Augusto Aixelà asked. "If you leave, what will happen to the old people's home?" "Someone far worthier than I will carry it on," Sister Consuelo said. "You know that's not true," he replied; "there's nobody with your ability or enthusiasm, and there's nobody I would move heaven and earth for as I have done for you." "Well then, there'll be no home," the nun said coolly. "It's a shame, but something far more transcendental is at stake." Augusto Aixelà retorted: "More transcendental for whom? For you, or for those old people you were so concerned about a month ago, and who you are so calmly jettisoning now because your integrity is in danger? Could it be that your famous project was nothing more than a means to ingratiate yourself?" "Don't talk nonsense," the nun butted in, "you know very well that nothing worthwhile can be bought at such a price." Augusto Aixelà's eyes shone with indignation. He took a step towards her, she backed away, but he went no closer. "Why do you talk about paying a price?" he said. "Have I ever asked you for anything?" She lowered her gaze and shook her head. He continued: "What are you so afraid of? Only of facing up to yourself: that's what you call the price you have to pay. The need to climb down from the pedestal you're on and accept that you have weaknesses too. The truth is, we're all human, and we cannot achieve anything worthwhile without paying the price of accepting ourselves for the weak creatures we are. Even Jesus Christ had to pay the price in order to carry out his mission as redeemer: he became a man, suffered, was tempted, and was frightened just like you." He took another step towards the nun. This time she did not move, but lifted her eyes and fixed them on him. Heavy teardops ran down her cheeks and her lips began to tremble. She whispered: "Be quiet, you are the devil himself." He burst out laughing: "The devil? That's a good one! Am I the one who is doing the tempting? Isn't it you who is tempting me? I didn't go to your cell to seek you out, and it wasn't me who made you come here today. Why have you been coming here if I am the devil? And why did you always appear on your own? You said no-one could accompany you because there was so much work at the hospital. Do you think I don't know that in your blessed hospital there are thirteen nuns for less than half a dozen patients?" Sister Consuelo silenced him with an abrupt gesture. "Save your breath. I can't hear you and I'm not listening. But don't worry, it's obvious you are not the devil, because if you were you would know that it's not your words that will be my downfall." No sooner had she said this than she rushed over to him, and flung herself into his arms, so violently he almost fell.

Half an hour later Sister Consuelo was still lying on the sofa in the study, her eyes half-closed, stubbornly silent. Whenever she looked up she felt as though she could sense the disapproving stares at her ravished womb from the truncated sculptures on the walls. Augusto Aixelà was standing leaning against the table, smoking. He broke the silence to say: "I thought you nuns had shaven heads."

These first words were so flippant that they had the effect of calming her down. "We used to," she replied: "but during the Civil War a lot of nuns trying to flee from the butchery were recognised because of this unusual feature and paid for it with their lives. Ever since then we have been permitted to wear our hair like this." She stroked the back of her neck and murmured in the same tone: "What will become of me now?" "Don't be upset about it," he said, "nothing happened here. Didn't you say you went to confession every day? By this time tomorrow you will have received absolution for your sin, and you have your whole life in front of you in which to be virtuous and enjoy your old people's home; after all, there is no reason now why you should give up the idea." Before she could reply there was a loud knocking at the door. "Who's there?" the landowner roared. Without answering the question or waiting for any kind of permission, Pudenciana pushed open the door and poked her head round. Taken by surprise on the sofa, Sister Consuelo gave a startled shriek. The housekeeper was left momentarily speechless, but soon recovered and said: "Forgive my intrusion, but the Civil Guard sergeant would like to see the master." "Tell him I can't see him today, but that tomorrow I'll definitely go to the guard post." "But he says that the day before yesterday you invited him to come and eat some of your special ham, and also that there's something extremely urgent he has to tell you." Augusto Aixelà stubbed out the cigarette in an ashtray with feigned exasperation, because in fact this unexpected visit gave him the opportunity to leave a lot of questions unanswered. "All right," he growled, "I'll be out in a second." After Pudenciana had left, Sister Consuelo said: "To gain God's forgiveness one has to repent for what one has done, and I will never ever repent for this, so I am lost." Augusto Aixelà stared at her for a few moments before replying: "Don't worry about these things, woman, there'll be plenty of time to talk them over more calmly later on. For now, you'll have to hurry: it'll soon be dark, and as you've heard, the sergeant is waiting to see me – I don't expect you want him to catch us like this." As soon as she had tidied her clothing, he took her to the curtain leading to the garden. "Go out round that side of the house and no-one will see you," he said. He was about to open the door, but she put her hand on the latch and said: "Wait, there's something I have to know. Don't lie to me: do you love me?" "Of course I do," he replied, "why do you ask?" She sighed and said: "I thought that once you had got what you wanted you would lose all interest in me." "Don't be such a child," he scolded her. "Will you always love me?" "Yes." "In that case, I'll come back tonight," she declared. "I'll be waiting for you," he said. The sun is going down, and with it my sense of shame, she thought when she found herself alone out on the veranda bathed in the golden light of sunset. Hail Mary full of grace, the parrot screeched when it saw her.

"I will not be coming to the refectory or to prayers tonight," she told the Doorkeeper when she reached the hospital. "Tell Mother Millas to take charge of everything, I don't want to be disturbed for any reason whatsoever." The nun looked down at the floor and said: "The Civil Guard sergeant was here. When he saw you weren't in, he said he would call back later. What shall I tell him if he comes?" Not only does he always pop up at the wrong time, he manages to be everywhere, thought the Mother Superior, what a nightmare! Out loud she said: "I've already told you I don't wish to see anyone, sister, don't question my orders."

Alone in her cell, her mind was prey to the wildest swings of emotion. She went from joy to despair in a moment; and no sooner did she fall into a listless stupor born of the emotional and physical impact she had suffered only a few hours earlier on the study sofa than she suddenly felt possessed by a tremendous energy that forced her to stride up and down the narrow cell and to kick her feet in the air to relieve some of the tension. She found the conviction that she had surrendered body and soul to the man she loved unbearable, yet she was desperate to run back to him and do so again. She felt an overwhelming desire to give herself to him, which all the human and divine obstacles only served to accentuate. Several hours went by in this kind of delirium, while she waited for the nuns to settle down for the night so that she could slip out of the hospital without being seen. The distant murmur of prayers and chants from the chapel exasperated her. Are those silly geese never going to leave off singing? she said to herself. Then, shocked at her own baseness, she covered her face with her hands and begged God not to abandon her at this decisive hour.

As the sound of voices died down, and then the noise of footsteps and the other muffled indications that the nuns were retiring for the night, Sister Consuelo decided to leave her cell. The darkness proved no obstacle to her, since she had studied the layout of the hospital in minute detail for her planned reforms, and was now able to find her way blindfold through the maze of rooms, corridors and stairways. She reached the entrance hall without a problem: in a niche, a votive lamp was burning in front of a statue of the madonna. There's no need for you look at me like that, the nun whispered to the statue, I know I am going to commit the worst of all possible sins – all I ask of you is that my unworthiness does not harm the hospital in any way. She opened the door with her key, went out, locked the door behind her, then threw the keys in through the peephole. The Provincial Superior already has my letter; when they tell her I disappeared leaving the keys behind, she will understand, she said to herself as she slowly emerged from the building's vast shadow. There was no moon, and the faint gleam of the stars barely permitted her to see more than an arm's length ahead; she regretted not having brought a candle. She was just thinking this when a dark figure holding a lantern emerged from the undergrowth that grew on either side of the road. At the sight of this apparition, she could not contain a startled scream. The strange figure also cried out in alarm, and the light nearly fell to the ground. Then the person recovered, and said: "Don't shout, sister, and don't be afraid, I'm not going to hurt you." As he said this, he shone the lantern light on his own face and smiled: the dim glimmer of light gave his features a ghostly aspect. "My name is Hilario," he went on, and humbly took his cap off. "I'm a shepherd, born in this village, and an honest man, even if not the brightest. I left my flock in their fold tonight to come and look for you." "For me? Are you sure it is me you are looking for?" the nun asked him in bewilderment. The shepherd nodded and pointed to the huge shadow of the hospital with his crook. "I've been waiting for you for almost two hours; I tried to get in, but the door is locked and bolted." "The hospital door is never shut to anyone," the Mother Superior replied. "It was for me today," the shepherd said, "otherwise, why would I be waiting outside?" Then, before the nun could protest, he went on: "There's someone who needs help, and I've come to take you so you can cure that person." "Is this person too sick to be brought to the hospital?" "That's impossible, sister, don't ask me any more," Hilario hissed. "But if it's such a serious case, why are you skulking out here? Don't you know to ring the bell?" "I couldn't," said the shepherd, "nobody must know I am here except you. I didn't want to climb in the window so as not to intrude upon your enclosed order; that's why I was waiting out here, praying to the Virgin that you would come out." Sister Consuelo was thoughtful for a while, then asked: "Who is this person who is so sick? Your wife?" "No, thank Heavens, I'm not married," said Hilario. "A relative?" "Yes, that's right, a cousin of mine." "What's wrong with your cousin?" "I can't tell you that either," the shepherd replied, "all I can say is that you must come with me, because if you don't, he'll die." "Why me and not a doctor?" "It has to be you or no-one," the shepherd repeated, "don't ask me any more questions." "I don't know very much about medicine," the nun warned him. "You'll know enough," Hilario replied, "if we don't waste any more time." "I'll need the first-aid kit." "There's everything you'll need where we are going to," the shepherd told her, "but you can't go dressed like that." He bent down, fumbled among the bushes he had been hiding in, and took out a bundle which he handed to Sister Consuelo. "Put these on." She glimpsed inside the bundle and by the light of the shepherd's lantern saw some used woman's clothing made of rough material. "Don't worry about putting them on, I'm not going to look," the shepherd said, "and even if I did, the night is so pitch-dark I couldn't see a thing." Seeing that she was still hesitating, he added forcefully: "Sister, do as I tell you quickly, and don't ask anything more."

7

THE SHEPHERD walked quickly and confidently over the rough ground, whose details he seemed to know like the back of his hand. The nun could barely keep up, and had to rely on him for help at every moment. The shepherd took her respect-fully by the arm and helped her round every obstacle with surprising ease: it was plain this was what he did every day with the animals in his charge. After about an hour's walking they came to a clearing in the wood; the shepherd lit a match, then immediately put it out. The nun asked him what he was doing. "It's a signal," the shepherd said. "Now we have to wait." The Mother Superior took advantage of this halt to ask him: "Haven't you and I met before? I think I know your face." "I don't think so," the man replied, "I'm always in the fields with my sheep, I rarely go down to the village, and still less to the hospital, thank God." He had scarcely finished saying this when a short stocky man with a pronounced limp came into the clearing. "Is this your cousin?" the nun wanted to know. "He is that," said the shepherd, "but he's not the one who is sick; this one goes by the name of *lo coix*." The new arrival removed his cap and held out a rough hand to the nun. "I'm *lo coix* and I'm grateful that you came." While she shook his hand, Sister Consuelo was straining to try and make out his features in the darkness; it was then she noticed the shotgun slung across his back. The shepherd bid them goodbye: "Good luck, sister, good luck, *coix*," he said, before vanishing silently into the undergrowth.

"Have a rest for a while if you like, sister," *lo coix* said, pointing to the mountainside rising in front of them. "We have a good bit of climbing to do." "I'm not tired," Sister Consuelo replied, "but I'm not used to climbing mountains either, I don't know if I'll be able to." "If I can, with my one leg and a half, you'll have no problem with those two sturdy legs of yours." When she heard this comment, Sister Consuelo remembered that the skirt she was wearing only came down to just below her knees. "Let's go," she said. The man unwound a length of rope he had been carrying, tied one end around his waist, and the other round hers. "This way if one of us puts a foot wrong, we're both for it," he joked. "What time is it?" Sister Consuelo asked after they had reached the top. "A little after two, I reckon," said *lo coix*, staring up at the stars twinkling in their thousands high above them. Sister Consuelo sighed. "Is there a long way to go?" "No, we're almost there," *lo coix* replied: "You're very strong and agile, sister; and brave into the bargain. It's a shame there aren't more women like you on this earth."

They walked for a while longer until they caught sight of a stone hut at the top of a slope. Two armed men stood guard outside the door, and a few yards away half a dozen others were sitting in a circle round a campfire. The hut looked abandoned: there were gaping holes in its walls, the roof was missing, and the window frame hung loosely from its hinges. "Go in, sister, and don't be afraid," *lo coix* said. "I'm not afraid," the nun said. Inside she found a man sitting close to some embers burning on the floor. He turned when he heard the door hinges creak. "I knew you would come, sister." "Are you the sick man?" Sister Consuelo asked. In response, the man lit a large candle with a brand from the fire. The greenish glow illuminated his pallid features. "So!" the nun exclaimed as she recognised the man, "you're the famous bandit, are you?" "Don't

77

be frightened," the brigand said. "I'm not frightened," the nun replied once more, "I'm surprised to see you, that's all: though I had realised you weren't such an idiot as you made out." The bandit gave a laugh. "And you're not as clever as you think," he said. "I'm no idiot, but the gardener at the Aixelà house is one all right; you were meeting two people, thinking we were one and the same." It took some time for this to sink in, but then Sister Consuelo said: "Don't tell me that the gardener is a cousin of yours as well." The bandit sniggered as though applauding his ruse: "Yes, and so are the shepherd and *lo coix*. For centuries, this village was cut off from the outside world, and the people here intermarried, so now we are all cousins and look alike. Thanks to that I can go anywhere freely: all I have to do is change clothes with someone else so that I can take their place without the Civil Guard or the rich so much as noticing: to them, we are all the same. As you can see," he said sarcastically, "they'd save themselves a lot of trouble if they paid us more attention, but it is in their nature to make use of people without looking us in the face." All of a sudden he shivered with cold, and wrapped himself more tightly in the blanket covering his shoulders. "Aren't you going to help me?" he asked. "Yes, but first finish telling me what you were doing at the Aixelà house. Were you planning to kidnap him?" The bandit burst out laughing again and said: "Kidnap him? No, what for? That fellow has no relatives or friends: nobody would pay a cent for him; in fact, there are probably lots who would be glad to see the back of him. I was only planning to rob him. I had heard that there is a very valuable art collection in the house, and I thought it would be better off in my hands than in that scoundrel's, so I took my cousin the gardener's place for a few days and found out where everything is kept, and what security measures they take or think they are taking; I also made myself a copy of the house keys, as you can see." He pointed to a corner of the hut where there was a sub-machine gun, ammunition, half a dozen grenades, and several other objects: among them the nun could make out a metal ring about six inches in diameter, from which hung a whole bunch of keys. "With these, there's no door in the whole village that can withstand me," the bandit said proudly. "I can even get into the hospital if I feel like it. But don't worry, I wouldn't dream of doing so." "It would be better for you if you did, because you're shivering with fever," Sister Consuelo replied. "It's the chill of the night air," the robber protested. "Don't be such a fool, everyone who's ill says the same thing, as if the problem will go away if they lie about it. Where does it hurt?" The bandit pulled up the blanket and stretched out his left leg; the trouser was torn, and a bloody bandage covered his thigh. Sister Consuelo brought the lamp up close and examined his wounded leg. "What was it?" "A bullet," the bandit replied. "By a stroke of luck it went right through without smashing the bone, but I can't move my leg or stand on it." "Yes, and it'll be a miracle if you don't lose it. Who bandaged it for you?" "The men you saw outside." "It shows," the nun retorted; "where are your medicines?" The bandit pointed to a bundle, inside which the nun found surgical equipment and medicines snatched without thought from raids on chemists or first-aid posts. She began to cut through the bandage around the outlaw's leg with a pair of scissors, but this proved so painful to him that she had to stop and call for *lo coix* to come and hold him still. When she had finished she said: "Put some water on to heat in a clean pan, and let it boil for ten minutes at least. I'm also going to need penicillin – send Hilario to the hospital to get some. If they ask him any questions, tell them I sent him." The man looked at his leader, who nodded. "I trust you," the bandit said after the other had gone out. "What choice have you got?" the nun said. "I'm talking seriously, I knew the moment I saw you that

79

you were a saint." "See? You're delirious," Sister Consuelo replied. "I know why you went to Augusto Aixelà's house," the bandit went on, ignoring the interruption. "I heard part of what you were talking about, and Cootie Pudenciana told me the rest: your idea for an old people's home, it's a good deed. My mother," he continued after a pause, "will soon be eighty, she's almost blind, and has no-one to look after her. She worked all her life from dawn to dusk and now she has nobody even to do the cooking for her: she's a sad case." "Sadder still because she has a renegade like you for a son," the nun retorted. "If you're so worried about your mother, what you should do is go back to look after her and change your ways." "Change my ways?" the bandit said sarcastically. "Ha, there's no way they would let me. And as for my mother," he added, "I know she's proud of me. She doesn't say so, but she is." He fell silent for a while, lost in his own thoughts; but then, taking up the thread of his conversation again, he went on: "You have a noble soul, but you're knocking at the wrong door. Augusto Aixelà, if you'll pardon the expression, is a bastard and a miserable wretch. He'll make a fool of you and won't give you a penny. All the rich are like that; otherwise they wouldn't be rich. I've robbed a lot of them so I know them well: you learn a fair deal of psychology through stealing. When they're staring at a loaded shotgun, people are more honest than in the confessional, sister, believe you me." "Just you lie still and don't talk such nonsense," said Sister Consuelo. "It's not nonsense," the bandit replied, "it's the plain truth, but you don't want to hear it, because you're completely taken in: that fop has turned your head with his ridiculous ways and his supposed generosity. It's all a fake: believe me, sister, that man is not for you, so don't give your heart to him; give him whatever else you like, that's your business, but not your heart, if you don't want to lose it forever." The nun stared at him in utter amazement. "What on earth are you talking about?" The wounded man smiled ruefully and replied: "About what I've seen and what I know: to be a good outlaw you have to be well informed, and I am. Look at this." He twisted and turned until he succeeded in pulling a dirty, crumpled envelope from his trouser pocket. He showed it to the nun, who immediately recognised it as the one she herself had written. "Where did you get that, you thief?" she exclaimed. "You gave it into the postman's hand," the bandit replied, "and he handed it to me. It's as easy as that." The nun made as though to grab the letter, but he was too quick for her and pulled his arm away. Sister Consuelo burst into tears, sobbing: "That is a confidential letter written to the Provincial Superior; you have no right to know what is in it." "Don't worry, sister," the bandit said, "only you or I know what's in the letter, or even that it exists, and I know how to keep my mouth shut." As he said this, he tore up the letter, then threw the pieces of paper into the embers. For a brief instant, the flames from the paper lent a ruddy glow to his gaunt face. "Your place is not behind the bars of a convent, but running an old people's home," the outlaw muttered as the last glimmer died away, "you owe me that favour."

In the distance the howling of a dog or perhaps a wolf could be heard. The nun had washed and disinfected the bandit's wound, and given him a sedative. Now he was asleep next to the fire; although the blanket was drawn up to his chin, his teeth were chattering incessantly. From time to time the hut door opened and *lo coix* peered in, stared at his leader for a while, then asked softly: "How is he?" "He's resting. What about the penicillin?" "Hilario is not back yet." "What time is it?" the nun wanted to know. Left alone again with the wounded bandit, Sister Consuelo nodded off. "I'm thirsty." When she heard this, the nun woke with a start, as though she felt guilty at having drifted off to sleep. She crossed herself automatically, then gave him something to drink. "I feel much better," he said, but when Sister Consuelo touched his forehead, she could tell it was bathed in cold sweat. "This will teach you not to go getting into trouble," she said to him gently. The outlaw smiled. "I'm no good for anything else," he said, "I was born bad, and society made me even worse." "That's a convenient excuse!" Sister Consuelo said. "It's not an excuse, sister, that's the way the world is; it turns good people into bad, and only gives those who are already bad all the more reason for being so; and that's the truth of it. Forget what they've taught you in the convent," he went on, "and take a good look around you, look at the way things really are. Poor little defenceless birds get eaten by hawks, but nothing eats the hawks; nature is cowardly and ruthless, and so is mankind. Laws are made by the rich to keep the poor in their place and to safeguard their own privileges. The rich are not bothered how harsh those laws are: they have no pressing needs, so they have no cause to break them. It's easy to be a millionaire and to say: a hundred years in jail for anyone who steals ten miserable coins. The police and judges are there to serve the rich, and the less said about the holy church the better: priests are the buffoons of the powerful; bishops are balloons blown up with their own hot air, and the Pope in Rome, with all due respect, is a crazy old whore." "If you carry on saying such filthy, impious things," the nun butted in indignantly, "I'll leave and let your men take care of you." "I'll say no more so as not to offend you," the outlaw said, "but I am sure that deep down, you believe the same as I do." "The only people who believe the same as you are four poor simpletons," she retorted, "and look where it's got them. Anyway," she went on, "I am convinced that you are not as bad as you like to pretend." "You think that because you are a saint, and have no knowledge of the world or of men," the outlaw replied. "I know enough to know we should not judge each other," said the nun. The bandit was quiet for a while, but just when it seemed he had let the matter drop, he suddenly continued, as if he were pursuing the thread of his own thoughts out loud: "To escape from the pit of misery and brutishness that fate had consigned me to, I took up arms in the Civil War when I was still only a child. Naturally, the outcome of that war only made things worse for me: at the end of three years' suffering I was as destitute as I had been at the start, and to top it all, I was fugitive from a justice which obeyed no other ideal than that of the victors' desire for blood. Faced with the hardships of exile I swore I would come back, not for vengeance, but for justice. Like an innocent, I thought the dispossessed would flock to my banner. But in reality, only half a dozen illiterates have chosen to follow me, and with them I spend my time stealing money from other unfortunates who probably need it more than I do. Yet that has been enough for me to be declared an outlaw and a terrorist: anyone and everyone has the right to shoot me as if I were vermin. So you see, sister, what a rough deal you get if you are born poor in this stinking country."

At four in the morning *lo coix* came in. "Hilario should have been back over an hour ago," he said with a worried air. "If he's fallen into the hands of the Civil Guard we'll have to get out of here." "There's no question of that," said the nun. "This man is in no state to be moved, except on a stretcher to be taken to hospital. His situation is critical; he needs the penicillin at once. If Hilario doesn't re-appear I'll go and fetch it myself." "No, you are not leaving here," *lo coix* said threateningly. "Calm down," the bandit ordered: "there's no need to be alarmed. Even if they've caught Hilario, he'll never give away where we're hiding, and if he does, it's no matter:

83

the Civil Guard will never risk coming into the mountains. They need the army's help to dislodge us from here, and they won't get that despite the fact that Augusto Aixelà, with all due respect, goes to Madrid every month to lick the minister's boots. We're safe here," he went on, "and as for the penicillin, there's time enough to take that. I have no intention of dying just yet." "What d'you think, sister?" his companion asked. "I don't know why you're so interested in my opinion, if you never listen to what I say," Sister Consuelo said. "I don't know much about medicine, and I don't have any equipment. If we don't act quickly, the infection could spread through his body. A doctor should see him and, if necessary, operate on him." "So he can chop my leg off?" the bandit protested, "I'd sooner die." "It won't come to that," *lo coix* interjected. The nun passed him the waterjug. "Boil some more water," she said, "I'll change his bandages." As she was doing so, she noticed that his leg was showing the first signs of gangrene. "Is something wrong?" the wounded man asked. "No," she lied, "it doesn't look too bad, but we need the penicillin at all costs." "I can't feel anything from my knee down," the bandit told her. "That's because of the sedatives," the nun said, and then to change the direction of the conversation, she asked: "How were you wounded?" "It's one of the risks of my profession," the bandit explained. "I went into Bassora and on the way back we ran into the Civil Guard. Because of the torrential rains, the stream was in flood and we couldn't cross it. We had to follow the bank until we reached the bridge, which gave the Civil Guard time to catch up with us. I had a hard job getting out of there." "Why did you go to Bassora?" "I had some business to do at the bank," the bandit said. "I can just imagine what kind of business," the nun said with a laugh. The outlaw grinned: "You're mistaken, I went to carry out a strictly legal transaction at the bank – a transaction which concerns you, by the way. In the past few months," he went on before she had time to express her surprise, "things had been going well for me, so I decided to invest the money I had accumulated as wisely as I could: after all, it is not much use to me personally." He coughed, then continued: "A cousin of mine works in a bank in Bassora: he explained to me how to perform the transaction, and now it's done. By now, if the bank has carried out my instructions, you should have received the transfer of the sum of two million pesetas to help finance your old people's home. When they see you've raised that much capital, the authorities will have to loosen their purse strings. It goes without saying," the outlaw continued, "that nowhere does it state where the money came from; nor is there any way of finding that out. I would also have preferred to keep the secret so that you would never have known who the donor was; but since you brought the matter up and since destiny has brought us together tonight, I could not resist telling you." He ended by saying: "There's no need for you to thank me." Sister Consuelo stared hard at the bandit to make sure he was not lying, and could see a gleam of undeniable, passionate sincerity in his eyes. "I can't believe my ears," she murmured. "But it's true," the bandit replied, "and my leg here is proof of it. As you can see, nobody can deal with banks and escape unscathed." "You know I can't accept that money," exclaimed the nun. "You can't refuse it either," the outlaw said: "it is the gift of an anonymous benefactor to the religious community you are part of: it is not for you to decide either to accept or reject it. And even if it were," he went on, "why not take it? The home is a noble idea, and I want to be associated with it in some way or other. I have not had many opportunities to do good in my life, so perhaps when the hour of judgment comes, God will remember this one and save my soul." "Don't joke about these things!" the nun protested, "salvation cannot be bought, and still less with stolen money." "Ah, sister, that is not what the church preaches when it is trying to woo the rich," responded the outlaw. Then after a long pause, he added: "But I won't lie to you. It's true that the home seems a noble idea to me, but that isn't the reason for my acting as I did. The truth is, I feel a very special and very real affection for you: please, don't force me to say anything further. I know that in your eyes I am nothing more than a deplorable, corrupt character, but don't think that means I have no feelings." At that, he fell silent, and Sister Consuelo was left to think over what she had just heard. I don't know whether God is putting me to the test, or making fun of me, she pondered.

Day was dawning; the bandit had fallen into an uneasy sleep once more, and the nun sat shivering. The coarse garments she had been given to wear did not protect her from the cold mountain air or from the early morning dew that soaked her through. She tried to stir the remains of the embers with a stick, but only succeeded in raising a cloud of whitish ash and in waking the bandit with the noise. "Put my blanket round you, sister," he said, "it's all the same to me now." Sister Consuelo struggled to her feet and rubbed her stiff joints. "I'll go and see if *lo coix* has anything he can lend me," she said. The frost-covered grass crunched beneath her feet. "Hilario is not back yet," *lo coix* said when he saw her coming, "I don't like the look of it." "I'm freezing," moaned the nun. He took a bottle of brandy out of the pocket of his sheepskin jacket. "Have a drink; it'll warm you up. There's nothing else I can offer you." "I'm not used to drinking anything alcoholic, but I'll take the bottle with me: I think it would help revive our patient for the moment at least," the nun said, as she stepped back into the hut. Once inside, she uncorked the bottle and drank a sip of brandy straight from it, then immediately had to slap herself on the chest to prevent a fit of coughing. "You should join my band, sister," laughed the outlaw, "you have the spirit of a fighter." "I don't know how you can drink this rat poison," Sister Consuelo retorted, passing him the bottle. The outlaw gulped some down, then shuddered. "It warms the body, makes you forget your troubles, and gives you courage," he said; "what more could you ask?" "I'll make do with the first," replied the nun. "What would the bishop say if he saw you tippling like this?" the bandit asked her slyly. "I've no idea," she said. "I have," replied the other. "After all, he hasn't spent the night out in the open, and nothing is easier than to give sermons from a cosy bed." "That's enough, don't drink any more and don't try to convert me: I'm the one who should be giving you a sermon, and yet I haven't." "That's true," said the bandit: "you are wonderful. If you put away your habit and marry me, I swear I'll lead an honest life." "You're drunk already," the nun said, taking the bottle from him with the intention of giving it back to *lo coix*. But just as she was about to leave the hut, the door burst open and *lo coix* came in. The bottle fell to the floor and smashed to pieces. "Hilario is back," he said, "the Civil Guard was waiting for him outside the hospital. They caught him, made him tell them where we were, then cut off his ears and sent him to tell us that they're on their way." There was a silence, then Sister Consuelo blurted out: "Why would they warn us about an attack?" "To scare the men," *lo coix* replied. "As soon as they heard the news, they threw down their arms and ran to surrender." Sister Consuelo peered out of the window: the flat stretch of ground opposite the hut was deserted. "I thought you weren't afraid of the Civil Guard," she said. "Not of the Civil Guard," *lo coix* replied, "but now they've brought reinforcements: forest rangers, Falange party people from Bassora, and an infantry section. That bastard Augusto Aixelà has got his way, there's no point resisting." The bandit struggled to get to his feet, but was unable to. "You make your getaway," he said to *lo coix*, "I'll try to keep them entertained. If you go to ground by day and travel at night, you'll reach France in three days' time, but get a move on." *Lo coix* turned and hobbled off, skirting the mountainside. "Now it's your turn," the bandit ordered the nun. "Walk straight across the open ground with your hands in the air: I don't think they'll fire at a woman." "What about you?" Sister Consuelo asked. The bandit shrugged and said: "I'm ready; sooner or later it had to come. But don't feel bad about it; there's not much lost with my death, and there will always be my cousin the idiot and my other cousin the bank manager to carry on the line." "Don't talk nonsense," said the nun. "You can't escape, but you can give yourself up, as your men have done. You'll be tried, spend a few years in jail, then you'll be free again. They can't be too harsh on you – after all, you haven't killed anyone." "You're the one talking nonsense," he retorted, "they'll gun me down as soon as they set eyes on me." "No," Sister Consuelo insisted, "do as I say: we'll go out together. If you're unarmed and with me they won't dare shoot you." "Don't you believe it; first they'll gun me down, then you, and they'll say that you were killed by a stray bullet in the shoot-out." He had hardly finished speaking when several explosions close by echoed round the mountain. "What was that?" Sister Consuelo asked. "*Lo coix*," replied the bandit. "Do you think they've killed him?" "We'll never know, and you shouldn't worry about that now," the outlaw said; "try to save your own skin."

"Halt! Civil Guard!" "What on earth is that?" the nun asked, terrified. "A megaphone," the bandit replied, "they're here already: you see what happens with all this talking? We've lost our last chance: pass me my gun." "You're not thinking of fighting in this hole, are you?" "No; if they've got the infantry with them, they'll bring mortars," the bandit said. "I'm going out – perhaps I can take them by surprise and cross their lines." Sister Consuelo passed him the machine gun, and helped him stand. He pulled his revolver out of his belt and handed it to her. "Go to the window and cover me!" he told her. "But I've no idea how to fire this thing!" she protested. "All you have to do is pull the trigger," the bandit said impatiently, "fire three shots then fling yourself down on the ground; and make sure you shoot into the air, I don't want you to hit anyone by accident." Sister Consuelo ran to the battered window, and the bandit limped over to the door. Only a few yards from the hut they could see men running crouched over, then roll behind the rocks for protection. The birds had broken off their morning celebrations; a tense and fearful silence reigned over the mountain. Leaning against the doorframe, the bandit raised his machine gun and shouted: "Fire!" then pushed open the door and leapt out, shooting as he did so. Sister Consuelo peeped out of the window and fired her pistol too. It recoiled so violently she almost dropped it, but she grasped the butt more firmly and fired off another two shots. She was thinking: "How can I be a nun if I always do what men tell me to?" Another burst of machine-gun fire came from outside. The nun threw herself to the floor as she heard the volley of shots: a hail of bullets whistled over her head and smashed into the wall opposite the window. When everything was quiet again, she opened her eyes and lifted her head. Through the thick cloud of dust filling the hut she could make out the silhouette of the bandit swaying in the doorway. She dropped the revolver and ran to support him, but could not prevent him collapsing onto the floor. She knelt beside the wounded man and laid his head in her lap to cushion it. "Are you hit?" she asked, but the reply was obvious, because the bandit lay in a pool of blood, and his voice was almost inaudible. "Our plan was no use," he hissed. Sister

Consuelo searched for a rag to staunch the flow of blood. "Don't bother, sister," he said faintly, "just give me your hand, I don't want to die alone." "You're not going to die, they'll soon have the penicillin here," she replied, "but all the same, it wouldn't be a bad idea if you made an act of contrition." The outlaw shook his head and replied: "No, sister, I don't repent for anything I've done: if at all, for not doing more harm when I had the opportunity. I detest society, and I detest mankind. I would die happy if I could be sure that after my death there will be more floods and earthquakes, more fires and epidemics. I want there to be wars, massacres and killings; I want crime and misfortune to rule; men do not merit peace or mercy, and nor does God. A curse on this earth and Him who created it." "Take back what you've just said at once," the nun said, "it's absurd to let your resentment condemn you to hell." The bandit stared up at Sister Consuelo; as his eyes glazed over, he murmured: "I don't believe in hell, or in heaven for that matter; even if they do exist, I couldn't care less: I refuse to accept a system which rewards hypocrites and condemns those who are desperate." The hut had filled with men who were pointing their shotguns at the two of them. "Lower your guns," Sister Consuelo told them, "this man is dead, and I'm no threat to you."

8

THEY HAULED her roughly out of the hut. If she resisted or stumbled, they pushed and prodded her with their rifle butts to make her stand up and keep going. Finally, they stood her against a wall of rock and stepped back a few paces. The first rays of sunshine lit the scene. Just as they were about to shoot, a voice rang out: "Stop!" The officer in charge of the squad ordered them to lower their weapons, and turned to face whoever it was who had dared to interrupt the execution. Sister Consuelo recognised her saviour as Sergeant Lastre. The infantry officer, the local Falange chief, and the Civil Guard sergeant moved away to discuss the matter between them. From her improvised scaffold, Sister Consuelo saw the sergeant pointing at her time and again; she also thought she could make out the name of Augusto Aixelà. Then a sudden, obscene gesture by the sergeant led the Falange leader to exclaim: "Good God, who would have thought it!" The three chiefs looked at her with renewed interest and exchanged knowing looks. Eventually Sergeant Lastre left the other two, came to where Sister Consuelo was still expecting to be shot, and said to her: "Come with me, sister." Nobody tried to stop them as they left the scene of the brief battle and began their descent of the mountain. The morning mist lifted as they went, and they soon arrived at the clearing in the woods, where the forest rangers were guarding the troop vehicles. Sergeant Lastre helped Sister Consuelo into his jeep, started the engine, and within a few minutes they had reached

the main road. The sergeant asked her: "Tell me what happened."
"There's nothing to tell," the nun replied. "I was asked to look after
a wounded man, and I did so, not knowing who it was. But I must
say that even if I had known, I would have done exactly the same."
"I understand," the sergeant said. "What did the brigand tell you?"
"Nothing," replied Sister Consuelo. "He must have told you something," the Civil Guardsman said, "you spent the whole night
together." "I've already said, he told me nothing," the nun insisted,
"he was badly wounded and was feverish; he was delirious." "I
understand," the sergeant said again, "and that's what I'll put in my
report. I'll also try to make sure your name doesn't appear
anywhere; I'll simply say that when the terrorist was killed there
was someone with him who had been forced to attend him against
their will." The nun stared at the sergeant, but he had his eyes fixed
on the road, and his expression gave no hint as to what he might
be thinking. Sister Consuelo, keenly aware that she reeked of a
mixture of cordite and cheap brandy, muttered: "Thank you,
sergeant." The sergeant contented himself with a grunt. A short
while later, Sister Consuelo asked him: "Where are you taking
me?" "To the hospital, of course," he replied. The nun became
alarmed: "No, no, for the love of God, I can't go to the hospital,
not yet; take me to Don Augusto Aixelà's, I beg you." The sergeant
frowned, but said nothing, and at the next crossroads took the side
road leading up to the Aixelà house. When he arrived at the gate
he pulled to a halt and lit a cigarette. "I'll wait for you here," he
said, "don't be long." Too exhausted to argue, Sister Consuelo
simply nodded, climbed down from the jeep, and entered the
garden.

Pudenciana had got up at daybreak, sharpened a knife and chopped
the heads off two chickens. She was in the middle of plucking them

when she heard the clatter of guns in the mountains. She crossed herself, then immersed herself once more in her monotonous task until her attention was caught by the dogs howling. Someone has died, she thought; and the idea distracted her so much that one of the dogs took advantage to sneak off with the chicken gizzards before she noticed. Pudenciana went out into the garden. At first she could not think who the ragged, dishevelled figure coming through the gate might be: first she was convinced it must be a gypsy, then a beggar; and finally, she decided it was a woman who had recently risen from the dead. The face was bloodless and haggard, the mouth shrivelled, the eyes staring emptily; the figure walked with an unsteady gait, like a blind creature feeling its way across a terrain sown with obstacles; its clothes were covered with brownish stains, and were ripped and torn so much they were on the verge of indecency. The dogs were so terrifed by this apparition they forgot their task as guardians and began to whimper. As Pudenciana approached, the pathetic-looking figure halted and opened its lips, but no sound came out; then it spread its arms with the palms of the hands turned outwards, and it was this gesture which for some unknown reason made the housekeeper realise it was Sister Consuelo, and that the stains on her dress were in fact coagulated blood. She was overwhelmed by a profound sense of pity for this suffering, bewildered woman who had been the victim of so much bitterness, terror, and violence, and who managed to teeter just this side of a complete breakdown only thanks to a blind, stubborn determination. She ran to hold her; as she did so, the blood from the chickens that covered her apron mixed with that of the dead outlaw. "Who's done this to you, child?" she exclaimed, and the nun, as if the sound of the housekeeper's voice and sense of her comforting embrace had finally undermined her resistance, broke into sobs, while her body was shaken with such convulsions that the dogs, unable to recognise human conduct in such an extraordinary display, slunk away with their tails between their legs. Incapable of thinking of anything else to do, Pudenciana simply hugged the wretched nun ever more tightly, fearing that if she let her go she might fall and really hurt herself. Outside, Sergeant Lastre sat perched on his jeep smoking, pretending not to notice what was going on in front of his eyes, as though this women's business did not concern him. After a while, the sobbing quietened, her tears stopped, and bit by bit Sister Consuelo regained control of herself. She cleared her throat so that she could speak and whispered in the housekeeper's ear: "What about him?" Pudenciana did not reply for a few moments. Then she said: "He's gone. He didn't say where to, or for how long, but he took enough luggage to be away for quite a long time." "Didn't he leave anything for me? A letter perhaps?" Sister Consuelo asked, a futile ray of hope in her eyes. "He didn't give me anything," Pudenciana tactfully replied, "but come with me and look to see if there is any sign of one in the study."

Pudenciana's strong arms supported the nun's weak frame. As they rounded a bend in the path, they saw the gardener walking clumsily towards them. The tip of his tongue stuck out from between his lips, and he was carrying a rubber basket full of black earth. Sister Consuelo shuddered when she saw how closely he resembled the man whose death she had so recently witnessed. The idiot raised the basket to show the two women what was in it: edible fungus and mushrooms that the heavy rains had caused to sprout poked through the clods of earth. He laughed a slackjawed guffaw, as though this were the most hilarious thing in the world. The two women passed by without stopping, and his face fell.

When they reached the house, Pudenciana said: "You must be faint from hunger; sit down and rest while I fry you some black pudding and onion." "No, please," Sister Consuelo protested, "I don't want anything to eat." "You have to eat or you'll get ill," the housekeeper insisted; "wait for me in the study and I'll bring you something." She disappeared, and Sister Consuelo went into the study. She started to search frantically for a letter with her name on it, which might offer her some explanation and hope, but there was nothing on any of the pieces of furniture, and the drawers were all locked. Pudenciana came in with a bowl full of milk. "It's still warm, look; ten minutes ago it was in the cow's udder," she said. "Drink it, you'll see it slips straight down, and there's no better pick-me-up." Sister Consuelo did not have the strength to refuse her offer, so she drank the bowlful of milk and said: "Thank you, Pudenciana, now I'd like to be left alone for a while." As soon as the housekeeper left, the nun sat in the same chair she had sat in the first time Augusto Aixelà had received her in the house. How long ago was that? she wondered; it seemed like a whole lifetime. She closed her eyes, and felt that the room was spinning around, so she opened them again and stood up, struggling to keep her balance. Gingerly, she went over to the sofa where she had been violated the evening before: it was a worn, comfortable, leather settee, and she could not help noticing a large brown stain on it. The seal of my downfall, she thought. She knelt on the floor and licked at it, but there was only a sharp taste of dust and hide. She stood up rapidly, ran across the study to the veranda outside, and brought up all the milk she had just drunk. Mother of God! screeched the parrot when it saw her arched over being sick. The nun wiped her lips and chin with the palm of her hand, and carried on walking. The torrential rain had stripped the soil from the vegetable garden and ruined the crops. The dark water of the pond was overflowing the sluices. Sister

Consuelo came to a stop at the foot of the sluice and stared down into the depths of the water. Her body had begun to sway, when all of a sudden she heard a voice behind her saying: "Be careful, sister, though it may not seem so, that pond is dangerous." The person speaking came up and calmly stood beside her: it was Pepet, the estate manager. "Sergeant Lastre told me I would find you in the house," he went on, "so I said he could go on, and I would take you back to the hospital safe and sound." He winked at her and added: "Don't get me into trouble, will you?" Sister Consuelo took two steps back from the edge and tore her eyes away from the fascination of the unfathomable. "Don't worry about that," she said in a steady voice. "Look at all this mess," the manager said, casting an expert eye over the garden. He clicked his tongue and added: "First it's years of drought, then years of floods, it's always the same story, praise be." He took the nun gently by the arm, steered her away from the pond, and the two of them headed wearily back towards the house. The sky was clear, and birds hopped among the washed out vegetables and perched on the poles of the scarecrows.

"You will be interested to know," the estate manager began in a studied tone of voice, "that late last night Don Augusto Aixelà came to my house. He got me out of my bed to tell me that Sergeant Lastre had been to see him earlier and informed him that the government had finally agreed to send troops to the area to flush the brigands out of the mountains. The sergeant also told him he had reason to think that the leader of the outlaws had been wounded in a recent clash with the Civil Guard, and that a joint operation involving the Civil Guard, army troops, and special forces from Bassora, was being planned for that very night. It seems that Sergeant Lastre then went to the hospital, intending to tell you the same thing and to warn you to keep the door locked and bolted and not to open it for anyone. He also gave instructions for no-one to leave after dark for whatever motive, but you were either not there, or could not see him for some reason, so that his warning, as you are well aware, went unheeded. For his part, Don Augusto told me that in view of this new turn of events, and since the bandits might possibly have supporters in the village, he had decided for reasons of security to leave at once, without telling anyone where he was going or for what length of time. He also said that he would in all likelihood be away far longer than usual, and instructed me to take charge of everything to do with the grape harvest this year. I was very surprised at this decision, which was so unlike him and so clearly not justified by the circumstances he gave as his excuse. I've known Don Augusto since he came into the world, so I knew there must be some other motive behind his flight, and I kept up my questions until I got the reply I was after. I didn't have to insist too much; men find it easy enough to talk about these things, that's the way they are. Of course," he hastened to add, "you have no need to worry. Your secret is safe with me; anything that happened between the two of you is none of my business; and what's more, however often we may meet after this conversation, I will never mention the matter again, and I ask the same of you. In fact, I have only brought it up because I feel it is my duty to inform you that Augusto Aixelà has left and has no intention of returning as long as you are here. I am saying it straight out because I am not used to beating about the bush and because I think you would prefer to know the truth than to go on building up false hopes for yourself. Besides," he went on, "I'm sure you're not surprised by what I'm saying. Neither your lack of experience in the ways of the world, nor the confusion you must be feeling after all that has happened to you can have prevented you from seeing just how far your relation was doomed to failure, even if any professions of love he may have made to you had been true." He paused, then added as an after-thought: "Augusto is a good lad, with a heart of gold, but he can't help what he can't help. Don't take it too badly: you aren't the first, and won't be the last. Forget him."

They had skirted the house and started down the path leading to the gate. Sister Consuelo stopped and turned back to look at the building. She gave a deep sigh, then found the strength to say: "It's humiliating to have to admit it, but I'm afraid I was even more innocent than you suppose: I believed in the sincerity of his words and his gestures. One afternoon he took me to the bedroom where his mother had died, and I saw genuine emotion in his eyes. Don Pepet," she went on forcefully, "men don't lie about things like that." The old man shrugged. "Some of them do," he said. "Augusto's mother is still alive and living in Madrid." The nun smiled sadly. "What a fool I've been!" she said. "Don't upset your-self about it," the manager advised her, "after all, it was almost bound to happen. There's never been a woman capable of resist-ing Don Augusto, he always knows how to tell them what they want to hear. He doesn't do it out of spite, it just comes naturally, it's a gift he has. You are an attractive, intelligent and forthright woman, and to top it all, a nun; Augusto is a hunter and a collec-tor: there was no way he could let such a rare specimen pass him by. He would have done anything to get you, you were lost however much resistance you put up, which wasn't very much in the end." "That's true," she admitted, "but am I so rare that he had to drag the Interior Ministry into my conquest?" "Oh no," the estate manager replied, "Don Augusto is a gentleman: he would never mix politics and his private affairs, or allow the public coffers to help him chase skirts; you surely never imagined that he was doing anything about your famous old people's home whenever

98

he went to Madrid, did you?" "Didn't he?" asked Sister Consuelo. "It never so much as crossed his mind," the estate manager replied.

The estate manager's green truck stood in place of the Civil Guard's jeep. They got in and travelled down to the hospital in silence. After they had arrived and the clanking of the decrepit engine had died away, the estate manager said: "Forgive me for talking to you in such a brutal way," but the nun answered: "No, I'm glad you did." She wanted to say something more, but her voice failed her. The old man patted her affectionately on the knee. "You're exhausted," he said, "sleep, eat, and in a few days you'll see everything in a different light; you'll probably end up laughing at what seems so terrible to you now." Sister Consuelo nodded and got out of the truck. The cat meowed from the back. The sister Doorkeeper had alerted the community, and they were all waiting in the convent hallway to give the Mother Superior a triumphant, joyous reception. "As soon as we heard the bandits had kidnapped you, we all congregated in the chapel, and prayed and sang that nothing would happen to you," they told her. Even the sick in the hospital had been pulled from their beds and taken to the chapel so that they could add their prayers to the nuns'. So much praying was bound to bear fruit, they thought, and so it had proved, praise be forever to the holy sacrament on the altar. The warmth of their reception moved Sister Consuelo, who had been worried about re-appearing in the convent looking like a disreputable drunk; she hugged her companions and shed copious tears. The estate manager's green truck disappeared banging and clattering, swathed in clouds of dust. The nuns' effusive welcome continued until the convent Bursar managed to separate Sister Consuelo from the noisy choir and get her alone in a corner. "I know you are exhausted, Reverend Mother, but I need to tell you something without delay." "Go ahead, Mother Millas." The Bursar, who until that moment had remained perfectly calm and collected, suddenly burst into tears. Through the thick glass of her spectacles, her tearful eyes loomed like goldfishbowls. "It's a miracle," she sobbed, "a true miracle; this very morning the bank manager came in person to tell me that an anonymous benefactor had donated two million pesetas to the community, to be used for the old people's home. It goes without saying that although he stressed that the donor wished to keep his identity absolutely secret, I would have to be very stupid not to realise who the altruistic and bountiful person was, just as I realise who it was who succeeded in touching the heart of that person with her quiet effort, her prayers and her example." The Bursar pulled a handkerchief from her sleeve, blew her nose loudly, then continued: "While I'm on the subject, I'd like to confess, Reverend Mother, that more than once I doubted the wisdom of your ideas and your behaviour. I will not deny that I often harboured malicious thoughts about you; I saw heterodoxy and frivolity in your expeditious methods, and I believed your conduct concealed a secret desire to win wordly praise. Now I understand how right you were in your way of going about things, and how wrong I was. I have been despicable and disloyal; I humbly beg you to pardon me and to punish me." Sister Consuelo hugged the Bursar and kissed her on both parchment-like cheeks. "Forget those minor details, Mother Millas," she exclaimed, "as you say, there has been a miracle, and now we have a lot of work to do."

9

THE CHANGES to the hospital were quickly carried out. Many prominent people from the world of politics and religion attended the opening of the old people's home, but Sister Consuelo was not among them. Shortly before the completion of the works which she had personally supervised in practice and which had in fact been financed thanks to her putting herself at risk, she was relieved of her responsibilities by her superiors and sent to a welfare centre at the opposite end of Spain. Far from feeling left out, Sister Consuelo saw in this transfer a well-intentioned wish to remove her from the temptation of pride, and obeyed gratefully. The centre she had been assigned to was poor and decrepit; thanks to her energetic diligence, within a short time it became a modern, active institution. After that, she was transferred several times, with equally successful results, so that Sister Consuelo's reputation as a founder of worthy projects spread far and wide. Thirty years went by, until one day as she was busy discussing technical details of her latest building project with some architects and builders, she suddenly passed out. "If the same thing had occurred ten minutes ago when we were up on the scaffolding, there's no telling what would have happened," she joked when she came round. "Yet again God has saved my life so I can go on serving Him." But the specialist who examined her did not agree. "Unfortunately, the first symptoms have come to light too late: there's nothing we can do." "How long do I have left?" Sister

Consuelo asked. The specialist shrugged. "Medicine is not an exact science," he said. "I need to know, doctor," the nun insisted, "I have a lot of unfinished business to attend to." "You have heard what the doctor just said," the Provincial Superior told her, "and nobody is irreplaceable. None of us can know the day or hour of our death, we only know we must always be ready to greet it with a spotless soul and a cheerful heart," she added sternly. The sick nun lowered her gaze as a sign of obedience, but she said: "For pity's sake, let me die in harness." "That's impossible," the Provincial Superior said sharply. Sister Consuelo did not reply: for several years now the Spanish government had regarded the magnificent social work the church had carried out for centuries with suspicion. Jealous of its prerogatives, the government regarded the church's selfless labour as interference in its affairs, and was continually hampering it. People like Sister Consuelo, who had once been regarded with veneration, were now an obstacle to church–state relations. Perhaps that was why the Provincial Superior was so pleased to see the back of her, Sister Consuelo reasoned. I am an embarrassment to my order, she told herself, disheartened. Out loud, all she said was: "God's will be done." The Provincial Superior's voice did not soften a bit when she added: "I have instructed that you be sent to a home where you will be well looked after. Rest, prepare yourself to die an honourable death, and make proper use of the remaining time that Almighty God sees fit to give you on this earth." The next day, Sister Consuelo left for her final resting place. She had not bothered to check where exactly she was being sent, but as they drew near, she recognised it immediately, and realised just how compassionate and kind the Provincial Superior had been despite her seeming harshness. "I always secretly carried this place with me in my heart," she commented out loud. The sister who was driving smiled. "It's only natural," she said, "this was the first old people's home you set up. That must be why the Mother Provincial decided you should be brought here to convalesce." "How do you know all this?" Sister Consuelo asked. "We were told about the home in the noviciate," replied the sister, keeping her eyes fixed on the highway road signs, "you were very popular among the novices, if you don't mind my saying so; as for that being the reason why you are being sent here, nobody told me, but I worked that out for myself." "How clever you nuns of today are!" Sister Consuelo exclaimed. "In my day we were all blithering idiots." "Now you're making fun of me, Reverend Mother," laughed the nun, but Sister Consuelo was no longer listening.

They had to cross Bassora; there was so much traffic in the town that the journey took a long time and exhausted the sick nun, who was in great pain. "Would you like us to stop for a while, Reverend Mother?" "No, child, it can't be much further, and I'd like to get there as soon as possible." They got lost in a neighbourhood full of tall modern buildings all of which looked alike; at ground level, there were small businesses or shops that were either empty or closed; there was no sign of any passers-by in the streets. Eventually they found a man carrying a suitcase and asked him how to get to San Ubaldo de Bassora. "This is San Ubaldo de Bassora," the man replied, "it used to be a separate village, but now it's part of the town of Bassora. Where do you want to get to?" They told him they wanted the San Ubaldo old people's home and the man, who said he knew it even though he was not from there, gave them the necessary directions. "How it's all changed!" Sister Consuelo exclaimed. "Before this used to be fields, the roads were not made up, and a car was a rare sight. Look," she said with almost childlike delight, "the village church is exactly where it used to be, but the square looks completely different . . . ah, now we're almost there, when we go round this bend we'll be able to see the towers of the old people's home." She was not mistaken, but the re-encounter left her disappointed rather than glad. The home had been altered in the mid-fifties with cheap materials, and had been poorly administered since then, so that, like the hospital of Bassora whose deficiencies had led to the building of the home in the first place, it had fallen into irreversible decline. Unable to bear the cost of such a ruin, the religious community had handed it over to the government of Catalonia several years earlier; on the wall in the entrance, instead of the statue of the madonna which had borne silent witness to the Mother Superior's conflict of passion, there now hung a portrait of Jordi Pujol.

When she heard of Sister Consuelo's arrival, the director of the home came out personally to greet her. She was middle-aged, and somewhat dry in manner, but nevertheless seemed courteous and efficient. She apologised for the lamentable state of the building, claiming that a series of strikes by the health workers had left the centre on the verge of catastrophe. Fortunately, the situation was getting better, she hastened to add, and trusted that the nun would have no cause for complaint. As she talked, she accompanied Sister Consuelo to her room; and then told her of the times and regulations in force in the home. "Doctor Suñé will come and see you today," she said, "he's our consultant and knows all about your case; if you need anything, don't hesitate to ask me." Sister Consuelo watched as the nun who had brought her unpacked her case and put her belongings in the wardrobe. "I'm sure you'll be well again soon, Reverend Mother," the nun said as she left, "we're all praying for you." Finally left on her own, Sister Consuelo stood staring out of the window: the poplar grove had been replaced by several blocks of flats, and the river had been turned into a canal and diverted so that there would be no more floods when there were heavy rains. She could still see the mountains in the distance though, and vividly recalled the day she had faced a firing squad on the top of one of those crags. Times change, hopes vanish, people die, only the mountains remain, she thought.

That afternoon Doctor Suñé came to visit her. "How are you? How is our patient today?" he asked. He was a young, jolly, round-faced man. "Doctor, tell me how much longer I have to live," she begged him, and seeing that he was hesitating, added brusquely: "and please don't tell me that medicine is not an exact science." "Do you think it is?" said the doctor. "I am only an ignorant nun," Sister Consuelo replied. Doctor Suñé opened the medical bag he had left on the table. "Do you know what a sphygmograph is?" he asked. "Of course, it's an instrument for measuring blood pressure." "You see? You're not as ignorant as you pretend: now roll your sleeve up and tell me how you learnt so much about medicine." "I've worked in hospitals all my life," the nun said. While they were talking, Doctor Suñé read the measurements from his instrument and noted them on a chart. "I've been told you were a nun, is that true?" "You've been misinformed," Sister Consuelo replied sharply. "I still am a nun." Then she smiled and said more equably: "I'm not saying these things to pick a quarrel with you, doctor, I simply don't want to be taken for more stupid than I am." "I'd already been warned that you were in a fighting mood," the doctor said, unperturbed, "why not disappoint them? Forget your hostility and let's be friends, what d'you say?" Then he added, "Until now, it's you who have looked after others; from now on, let the others look after you, will you?" He stood up to leave, but Sister Consuelo grasped his sleeve to keep him by her side. "Doctor, listen to me," she said, "don't think I'm concerned about dying now; I've lived a long life and I've been granted the privilege of doing a lot in it. Of course, it does not seem that way to me – I feel my life has gone by in the twinkling of an eye, and I think there are still many things I have to do but that is mere egotism and vanity. Although I believe in the afterlife, I would like to prolong this one indefinitely. I would like to live forever, like the most unenlightened atheist, but I know only too well that all of us, atheists or believers, are bound to die. I at least will do so comforted by the sure hope of a life beyond this one and, when all is said and done, what more is left to me in this world but the decay of my body and of my spirit?" Doctor Suñé stood listening to her in silence, bag in hand. "How long, doctor?" Sister Consuelo insisted. "A month at the most," the doctor said, "perhaps less; I'm not sure I'm doing the right thing by telling you."

In the weeks following this first meeting, it seemed that Doctor Suñé's predictions were being inexorably fulfilled. Sister Consuelo's general condition deteriorated visibly. She was, however, a model patient: she never complained and always had a cheery word for everyone. To Doctor Suñé's great surprise, she made no attempt to resist taking the numerous medicines prescribed whenever required to do so. She slept only a little, and then it was thanks to sedatives which during her waking hours left her lethargic and confused. Even though she had no appetite what-soever, she made great efforts to eat. "Life is a precious object God has granted us, and we must do all we can to preserve it," she would say. Naturally, none of the measures taken could halt the ferocious spread of the illness. "Praise be to God," she murmured each day as she became aware of the rapid deterioration of her faculties. She could no longer read even wearing glasses, and had to be aided by a nurse whenever she took the daily walk the doctor had prescribed. Sometimes this terrible draining away of her life was too much for her. "I'm sure that things weren't like this before, doctor," she said to him whenever his visits coincided with her moments of lucidity, "in the past, people lived and died without having to go through these terrible periods of transition; it is medical progress which has created this horrible situation." "Perhaps medicine has simply restored the natural order of things," Doctor Suñé replied. "If it takes years for the body and the brain to develop, it is only logical that they take some time to decay as well. The last years of the old are like the first that children live: it's cruel, but natural, and medicine did not invent human nature. It merely found it already existing, and tried to understand it, to adapt to its vagaries. It is God you must call to account, sister, not doctors." His patient would have none of it. "Why don't you admit that it is the doctors who have distorted divine creation," she retorted, pointing to the drip. "I refuse to believe this is the natural course of human life." "Nothing is natural in human life," the doctor declared, "we have to accept that evidence, but that doesn't mean we should throw in the towel." "Ah, doctor, don't make me go for any more walks, they exhaust me, and what use are they?" "Come now, sister, don't give up on the world of the living just yet, keep on fighting," Doctor Suñé insisted; "get out of bed, watch television, listen to the radio, get to know the other residents; don't you like playing cards?" "I've never played any games, doctor, I wouldn't know how to tell any of the suits in a pack of cards," the nun replied, "and I'm not used to being sociable. I don't think I've ever talked to anyone about anything that wasn't a specific matter." And yet in the end she gave way to the doctor's arguments.

"Everything you say to me is nonsense, doctor, but I don't have the time left to try to win an argument. Do as you think fit," she said to him.

One day, close to the limit that Doctor Suñé had predicted, Sister Consuelo realised that her end was near and said to him: "Doctor, you were right, it's all over. You have been a good doctor and friend, and I hope I have been a good patient. Now, though, I want you to forget your profession and my condition for a moment, because I'm going to ask you a great favour." Doctor Suñé stared hard at her. "Don't worry," continued the nun, "it's nothing against your or my principles; in fact, it's something very simple, almost childish. Look, close to here there's an old farm which according to what I've heard is still called the Aixelà house, even though it's now owned by other people. Do you know the farm I mean?" The doctor replied that he did, because he had visited it on several occasions. Sister Consuelo hesitated before she phrased her next question; finally she plucked up her courage and said: "Doctor, do you think there is any way I could visit it too?" Doctor Suñé did not hide his astonishment at such an outlandish request. "What you're asking is completely out of the question, sister. You know better than I do what kind of a state you are in physically." Sister Consuelo sighed and fell silent; the doctor put away the pen he had been making notes with on his pad. "Is this visit really so important for you?" he asked. All Sister Consuelo did was to close her eyes; a single tear rolled down the white wax of her sunken cheeks. "All right, if it doesn't rain tomorrow, I myself will take you to the Aixelà house," said Doctor Suñé, "but don't mention this to anyone, I don't want to create a precedent." That night Sister Consuelo prayed to God that it would not rain and that He might give her the strength to endure until the good doctor had fulfilled his promise.

The day dawned sunny. In mid-morning Doctor Suñé came into Sister Consuelo's room. Instead of his customary white coat he was casually dressed, in a tan suede jacket. He took a small bottle and a syringe from his bag. "I'm going to take you off all those tubes and give you an injection," he said, "you'll notice the effects straight-away, but don't get the wrong idea, it will only last a couple of hours." Exactly as he had said, as Sister Consuelo was crossing the entrance hall to the home, she felt strangely euphoric, as if she wanted to jump and dance, but her legs were so weak that she could barely shuffle along clutching at the doctor's arm. Through a glass door she could see a group of old people staring open-mouthed at a talk show on a silent television screen; a warm smell of soup wafting from the kitchen made her gorge rise. "I've got the car right outside," the doctor said, seeing her weaken. Once inside the car, he tightened her seat belt. "There's still time for you to change your mind," he said. Sister Consuelo shook her head, and Doctor Suñé set off.

There was little traffic, and they completed the journey in a few minutes. New buildings obscured the farmhouse, and Sister Consuelo was surprised to find herself suddenly outside the old gate. The wall and the grille had been conserved and probably even restored in recent years but, seen from outside, the garden looked abandoned. The farm, as Doctor Suñé explained, belonged to some people who were only there for a few days in the summer. The rest of the time a couple of caretakers kept out thieves and vandals; at one point there had been talk of converting it into a hotel, then a water sports centre, and finally a golf club, but none of these had gone beyond talk. He got out of the car, leaving the nun inside, and went to the gate, where he pressed the buzzer on the intercom several times. When he received a reply, he had a short dialogue through the apparatus. Still sitting inside the car with the seat belt on, Sister Consuelo could not hear what he was saying. The gate swung open automatically. "I called yesterday afternoon to say we were coming," the doctor explained as he turned into the drive, "the caretaker is expecting us." Sister Consuelo looked to right and left, confused: she was not sure whether it was the things around her which had changed or whether it was her memory which over the years had played tricks on her and constructed an unreal landscape. Everything looks smaller than I remember it, she said to herself, and uglier. The heather border which used to grow by the outside wall had gone, and the ground was now full of brambles and nettles. The track which wound its way between the trees had been replaced by a wide, asphalted drive, which led straight and unimaginatively up to the farmhouse. The trees in the garden had died or been cut down, and on the level ground by the house now stood a tennis court surrounded by a high wire fence. Withered flowerbeds were further evidence of the neglect the new owners left the farm in. The car came to a halt outside the farmhouse, and before they had time to get out, the caretaker came to meet them. He was a wary-looking Senegalese, who spoke Catalan correctly and fluently despite his strong foreign accent. He greeted the doctor courteously, and told him he had been telephoning Barcelona without success to see if he could find the owners of the farm, because he was not allowed to let anyone in without their permission. The previous owner, he explained, had collected works of art, and there were still some valuable pieces inside the house, which meant he felt a great burden of responsibility, because the new owner had given him strict instructions in this respect, on top of which, he added, the vulnerable position of black workers in Spain meant he had to take extra care. "I know that both you and the lady with you are of unquestionable honesty," he went on, "but anyone could accidentally damage one of the things, and if that were to happen, goodness gracious, I shudder to think what they would say." The doctor was about to argue the point with him, but Sister Consuelo stopped him. "It doesn't matter, doctor," she whispered in his ear, "just ask him if there is still a vegetable garden behind the house." "I should say so," the caretaker replied when the doctor conveyed this message to him, "and I look after it well. If you would like to see it, that's no problem, just so long as you don't step on anywhere that's planted."

They walked slowly round the side of the house until they reached the veranda. Up the hillside, which before had been sown with alfalfa and planted with vines, there were now several dozen white two-storey chalets. Each of them had a garage and its own garden, separated from its neighbour by a whitewashed wall, and in the middle of each garden swayed a tiny, bare tree. A huge board announced that this residential development was about to open; some of the chalets, it said, were still for sale. Sister Consuelo gave a deep sigh. "You're tired," said Doctor Suñé, "let's go back to the car." "No, no, we must see the vegetable garden, then we can go back," the nun insisted. "It's my responsibility to look after you," the doctor started to say, but Sister Consuelo interrupted him: "I absolve you from all such responsibility." "You don't know what you're taking on," the doctor muttered, "I'll help you go wherever you wish, but if you fall and break a bone, I'll break another one because you're so stubborn."

★ ★ ★

The vegetable garden had not changed. There was a smell of wet earth and freshly dug vegetables in the air. A dragonfly zigzagged past them, and somewhere in the distance a frog croaked. Doctor Suñé and his patient stood on the edge of the pond. Sister Consuelo stared down into the water for a while, then murmured, "This is where I wanted to come; we can go now." "I don't wish to seem indiscreet, but is there nothing you want to tell me?" Sister Consuelo smiled sadly. "I'm sorry, but I can't tell you the secret; all I can say is that it has to do with something which happened to me a long time ago, when I was a young woman. In those days I used to come to this house and knew the man who was its owner. I spent moments here which I now see as happy ones, and since fate has brought me to San Ubaldo again, I did not want to leave this world without returning here one last time." She looked down into the water in silence again, then added: "Would you believe me if I told you that I was once seriously considering throwing myself head-first into this pond?" The doctor said nothing for a while, then replied: "No, from the little I know of you, I would not be surprised; but can I ask why?" "Why I was going to throw myself in, or why I didn't in the end?" Sister Consuelo asked. "Which of the two questions would you be prepared to answer?" he said. The nun smiled: "Neither." The doctor smiled as well: perhaps due to the soft, filtered light in the garden, some of the harshness that the past few weeks of pain and desolation had brought to the nun's features had vanished, and her face looked gentle and serene. He glanced at his watch. "Now it really is getting late," he said.

On the journey back to the home, the nun asked Doctor Suñé how he came to know the farm. He told her that some years earlier, just after he had been selected for the position of doctor at the home, he had been to the farmhouse to attend its former owner. "He was an old rogue by the name of Augusto Aixelà de Collbató," he said, "perhaps he was the same person you knew." Sister Consuelo replied that it was indeed the same person, and begged the doctor to go on with his story. The doctor did so, saying: "At the time I met him, Augusto Aixelà lived on his own in truly disastrous circumstances: his health was poor, and he showed clear symptoms of senile dementia. His economic situation was no better. Apparently, he had once possessed a considerable fortune, which he had dissipated in the most stupid manner. His weak, libertine nature led him to surround himself with false friends, undesirable characters who abused his trust and involved him in ruinous business ventures. Bit by bit, his vices and the fraudulent deals swallowed up his inheritance. In the end, all he had left was the house, the garden and the vegetable patch, and all these were heavily mortgaged too. He survived a few more years by selling off his splendid art collection, the furniture and the valuable objects he had in the house, including a roomful of family portraits, but eventually, with misery staring him in the face, he had to give in, and reluctantly sold off all he still owned to settle his debts. Then, completely penniless, he went into the old people's home, where he lived on for a couple of years, during which time no-one came to visit him. He only had a few distant relatives, most of whom he had quarrelled with during his life, and whom he could no longer attract with the promise of a substantial inheritance. We never got on," the doctor continued. "Augusto Aixelà was an irascible, authoritarian old braggart. He treated the nurses badly simply because they would not let him feel them up; he was forever sending letters to *La Vanguardia* in Barcelona complaining without reason of the lack of hygiene in the home, about the food and the staff; and he would tell anyone who would listen that he deserved special treatment, because even though he might now not even be able to pay for his upkeep and had to depend on public charity, once upon a time he had paid for the refurbishment of the old hospital out of his own pocket." Doctor Suñé paused for a moment, then added: "He also used to say that he had made the gift to please a woman he had loved with all his heart, but who had not returned his love." When she heard this, Sister Consuelo, who had closed her eyes and seemed to have been lulled into sleep by the doctor's voice, shook her head and said with a smile: "He always was a great liar."

THE DAY after their visit to the Aixelà house, Doctor Suñé found his patient in a state of complete prostration. "I think we spent the last cartridge yesterday, sister," he said, "I'm sorry I let you talk me into it." The nun smiled at him. "You can't imagine how grateful I am for what you did for me, doctor." She confessed, took communion and received extreme unction, then fell into a coma. The director of the home informed the nun's family of her state, and two aged men who said they were Sister Consuelo's brothers arrived the same afternoon, just as she was breathing her last. When Doctor Suñé came to offer his condolences, they explained they had not seen their sister for many years, from the moment that as a child she had left the family home to become a novice. After entering religion, Sister Consuelo had cut all links with her family, they said, and since then they had only met perhaps four or five times, always at funerals. For this reason, they admitted, the death of their sister had not affected them deeply. In spite of this, during the funeral service the younger of the two could not hold back his tears on several occasions, and in the cemetery they were both visibly moved. Before leaving, they asked if any costs had been incurred by their sister's illness or burial, in which case they were more than willing to pay. They were told that the religious order would meet all the expenses. This reply seemed only to intensify their sense of loss. "Poor Constanza," they said, "she was our little sister, but we could never do anything for her, not even now."

That afternoon, as Doctor Suñé was preparing to go home after the funeral, a nurse gave him a letter which she said had been found in Sister Consuelo's room by the people who were cleaning and disinfecting it. Although it was the dead nun's personal property, the nurse added, it was in fact addressed to Doctor Suñé, so she had thought it best to give it to him directly without telling the director or the dead woman's brothers. Doctor Suñé told her she had done the right thing, and took the letter home, where he read it straightaway. It was written in a trembling, not always legible, handwriting. It said: "Yesterday afternoon, in the garden at the Aixelà house, you showed a natural wish to know why I felt so compelled to visit there when I was so to speak at death's door, and I found myself unable to respond sincerely to the generosity and kindness you had shown by accepting my request. The fact is that I refused to tell you what had once happened there out of a sense of shame that is even more absurd now, given that on that occasion this was precisely what I should have felt, but did not. What happened "the letter went on" is very simple: the Aixelà house was where many years ago I lost first my head and then my honour in the arms of a man for whose love I would gladly have abandoned my life of religion, if God had not blocked my way with His unalterable will." The letter, written with more haste than care – doubtless due to the urgency Sister Consuelo felt as her faculties faded – continued thus: "This took place during the year of the flood: following a lengthy drought, the skies opened and heavy rains devastated the region. Factories and houses were flooded in Bassora, many families were left homeless, and several people lost their lives in the catastrophe, but all that was the same to me, all I knew was that the breeze wafting in through the study window brought me the pure, blissful perfume of the flowers in the garden. Perhaps we could have been happy," the letter went on, "if all the elements of nature and a series of events as unexpected as they were terrible had not conspired to separate us. I did not go to meet him as I had promised that night because I became caught up in a bloody incident that still makes me shudder when I think of it, and this prevented me from fulfilling my promise and my most earnest desire. By the time I finally reached his house, he had gone. The rest of my life has been one long, silent falsehood: even after all these years I still find refuge in the warm memory of the only moment of intimacy I have known in this world. Without it, I do not know how I could have borne so much solitude. Now my end has come and the moment has arrived when I am to be called to account by the Almighty. I am fearful at the prospect; I have faith in His infinite mercy, but I tremble at the thought of His strict justice, which I have sought in vain to evade for so many years, confessing to my sin a thousand times, but never admitting my blame, because I am still there, bathed in the gentle light of that summer afternoon, in a turmoil but content, indifferent to everything else – even though I know full well that it is this proud and stubborn defiance which means I will be condemned." The final paragraphs of the letter, written when her strength was obviously ebbing away fast, were barely comprehensible. Some sentences or phrases seemed to have been written with a firmer grasp, but their meaning was still unclear. "Suffering, joy and passion are nothing but a dream," one part said, completely out of context. Another, in almost illegible lettering, apparently read: "I have always been terrified of eternity; I imagine it as somewhere immense, where the opportunity to re-encounter someone is rare; if this in fact turns out to be the case and we never meet again, I want you to know, my love, that I have always loved you and always will." This sudden, incoherent outburst was followed by a few more lines of scribble, as though the hand tracing them had continued with the mechanical gesture of writing even after the spirit guiding it had already crossed the boundaries of this world.

Finis

Peter Høeg

MISS SMILLA'S FEELING FOR SNOW

Translated by F. David

"A subtle novel, yet direct, clever, wistful, unforgettable"
RUTH RENDELL, *Daily Telegraph*

"It is extremely hard to put this long novel down and the excitement it engenders spills over into your time away from it . . . Peter Høeg's novel is already making for classic status"
PAUL BINDING, *Independent*

Peter Høeg

BORDERLINERS

Translated by Barbara Haveland

"It exerts the same chill grip on the imagination as its predecessor *Miss Smilla's Feeling for Snow*, posing questions and withholding answers with the same disconcerting skill . . . The power of the novel lies in the awesome truthfulness of the child's voice"
SALLY LAIRD, *Observer*

"The sustained intensity and brilliance with which the lives of these 'dark and dubious children' are captured is overpowering"
JOHN MELMOTH, *Sunday Times*

Boris Pasternak

DOCTOR ZHIVAGO

Translated by Manya Harari and Max Hayward

"The first work of genius to come out of Russia since the Revolution" **V. S. PRITCHETT**

"A book that made a most profound impression upon me and the memory of which still does . . . not since Shakespeare has love been so fully, vividly, scrupulously and directly communicated . . . The novel is a total experience, not parts or aspects: of what other 20th-century work of the imagination could this be said?"

ISAIAH BERLIN, *Sunday Times*

Giuseppe Tomasi di Lampedusa

THE LEOPARD

Translated by Archibald Colquhoun

"The poetry of Lampedusa's novel flows into the Sicilian countryside . . . a work of great artistry"

PETER ACKROYD, *The Times*

"Every once in a while, like certain golden moments of happiness, infinitely memorable, one stumbles on a book or writer, and the impact is like an indelible mark. Lampedusa's *The Leopard*, his only novel, and a masterpiece, is such a work" **BRUCE ARNOLD**, *Independent*

James Buchan

HEART'S JOURNEY IN WINTER

"I don't believe this country has a better writer to offer than James Buchan. I can't think of anyone who concedes so much of his own intelligence to his protagonists – doesn't mock or belittle them – and gives them so much world to do battle with"

MICHAEL HOFMANN, *London Review of Books*

"Like Conrad, Buchan sews thrilling biographical jackets for his characters, made from the threads of history"

JAMES WOOD, *Guardian*

Georges Perec

LIFE A USER'S MANUAL

Translated by David Bellos

"A dazzling, crazy-quilt monument to the imagination"

PAUL AUSTER, *New York Times Book Review*

"One of the great novels of the century"

GABRIEL JOSIPOVICI, *Times Literary Supplement*

Cees Nooteboom

THE FOLLOWING STORY

Translated by Ina Rilke

"Nooteboom is one of the greatest modern novelists"
A. S. BYATT, *Daily Telegraph*

"Nooteboom has shown himself a master of ironic wisdom, but also of elated, elegiac feeling. Intricately composed and finely translated, *The Following Story* will still be delivering after many readings – and on the first it is funny as well as affecting"
BEN ROGERS, *Independent on Sunday*

Aleksandr Solzhenitsyn

ONE DAY IN THE LIFE
OF IVAN DENISOVICH

Translated by H. W. Willetts

"A masterpiece in the great Russian tradition. There have been many literary sensations since Stalin died. *Doctor Zhivago* apart, few of them can stand up in their own right as works of art. *Ivan Denisovich* is different"
LEONARD SCHAPIRO, *New Statesman*

Richard Ford

THE SPORTSWRITER

"Richard Ford has wrought a pitch-perfect thing of wonder
. . . a brilliant elegiac novel"

DAN CRYER, *Newsday*

INDEPENDENCE DAY

"It is nothing less than the story of the 20th-century itself . . .
Ford has created an extraordinary epic"

PENNY PERRICK, *The Times*

Winner of the Pulitzer Prize for Fiction 1995

ROCK SPRINGS

"The first thing that needs to be said about this collection
of stories . . . is that the finest of them achieve luminous
moments, moments with the potential to change how the
reader sees and thinks"

JOHN EDGAR WIDEMAN, *New York Times*

Richard Ford

WILDLIFE

"His prose is strong, clear and satisfying, resonant with the bleak rhythms of unrewarded lives"

PENNY PERRICK, *Sunday Times*

THE ULTIMATE GOOD LUCK

"So hardboiled and tough that it might have been written on the back of a trenchcoat. A grand *Maltese Falcon* of a novel"

STANLEY ELKIN

A PIECE OF MY HEART

"Quality writing in the highest American tradition of Faulkner, Hemingway and Steinbeck"

PETER TINNISWOOD, *The Times*

SEPTEMBER 1996

To join the mailing list and for a full list of titles please write to:

THE HARVILL PRESS

84 THORNHILL ROAD
LONDON N1 1RD, UK

enclosing a stamped-addressed envelope